TEMPORAL GAMBIT

LARRY A. BROWN

TEMPORAL GAMBIT

Creative Arts Press

An imprint of Sienna Bay Press

P.O. Box 158582

Nashville, TN 37215

ISBN: 978-1-945527-41-8

Cover design by Elizabeth Mackey

Editing by Emerald Ink

To my wife Shannon, who has published many of her own novels. When I didn't think I could, she prodded me into writing my first work of fiction, encouraged me all along the way, and helped edit the final version. To her, my love and thanks.

August 8, 2059

"WHAT TIME IS IT?"

"6:23."

"How long has he been back?"

"A little over an hour. Don't worry; it looks like he's starting to wake up."

Martin heard voices around him. Familiar voices. His eyes fluttered open and squinted at the overhead light. He tried to focus on the shadowy figures hovering over him. "How long?" His throat was dry, his voice raspy.

"You've been gone about twelve hours in both your subjective time in the past and in present time," the blurry face above him said. "This corresponds to our calculations for when the temporal distortion wave would collapse. So we're quite pleased with the data for the initial jump."

"Welcome back, Martin. You've just traveled almost two hundred years and look none the worse for wear."

The speaker wore a stethoscope around his neck. "How do you feel?"

"Groggy … a bit hard to concentrate," he responded, rubbing his forehead. "But no pain. I can't remember what happened, though."

"That's to be expected. The effect of the stabilizing meds should wear off soon. This is why we insisted on using the cyber-chip to record your thoughts during the trip."

Martin found himself in a long, cylindrical tank half filled with a warm liquid. The hinged lid to the device lay off to one side at an angle. He was wearing a skin-tight outfit much like a scuba-diving suit but made of an iridescent material that shimmered in a rainbow of colors under the lights. It covered his entire body, including his head, leaving only his hands and face bare.

Gripping the sides of the tank, Martin pulled himself upright.

"Dracula rises from his coffin. Quick, where's the garlic?" That snide comment came from David Barton, the resident smart aleck, sitting at his computer surrounded by candy wrappers. David's ability to interject sarcasm into almost any situation was matched only by his expert programming skills.

Next to him were John Rey Bautista and Rosa Santos, the Chronos Project's theoretical physicists. They had joined the team after leaving top-secret work with the military. Both were Filipino, although their families had lived in the United States for several generations. They were a likable and cute couple, even though they had the annoying habit of conversing privately in Tagalog, which no one else in the group understood.

Dr. S.P. Hewes was the team's physician, responsible for the well-being of everyone but especially the time jumper. He had practiced medicine at the Mayo Clinic and Johns Hopkins for three decades before accepting his current position.

Finally, standing off in the corner was Andrea Carlton. She served as the official observer for the project's anonymous sponsor, reporting back on progress and overseeing the finances. Skeptical by nature, she had doubts about the entire business of time travel.

Glancing around the room, Martin felt grateful to work with this team of specialists. The Chronos Project had recruited the best of the best, which wasn't hard when you had a mysterious patron with seemingly unlimited resources.

S.P. helped Martin climb out of the pod, and Rosa handed him a towel to dry off. The liquid dripping on the floor made a slippery mess, but it was necessary to induce the state of sensory deprivation for the person inside the pod. Once the lid was sealed, all light and sound were eliminated, and the salt water solution created the feeling of weightlessness.

Why this experience was needed for time travel, Martin did not understand, but he trusted that his colleagues knew what they were doing. He left science to the experts while they left history to him — an equitable arrangement, in his opinion.

Andrea spoke up for the first time. "Very well. If you're

ready, why don't we download your personal log to determine if this huge financial gamble has paid off?"

Martin deposited the wet towel in the nearby hamper and made his way to the chair at the computer. David gave him a round electrode pad with a wire running from it, which he attached to the spot below his left ear where the cyber-chip had been implanted under the skin. The team all turned to the large monitor on the wall and watched as it began transcribing the log.

Chronos Project
Personal Mission Log: Dr. Martin Chamberlain
Departure date: August 8, 2059
Target destination: Gettysburg, Pennsylvania
Target date: November 19, 1863

HELLO, THIS IS MARTIN CHAMBERLAIN. I'M SPEAKING ... OR rather thinking these words as a permanent record of my first journey through time. I assume the cyber-chip in my head is working properly and preserving my observations of this trip for posterity.

I feel like Neil Armstrong when he walked on the moon ninety years ago, saying, "One small step for man, one giant leap for mankind." Hopefully, my experience of this historic event will be remembered as well.

The last thing I recall is S.P. — that is, Dr. Hewes, for the official record — closing the lid on the pod. Lying half submerged in the salt water solution, it felt like floating in the darkness and silence of space. I must have lost consciousness since the next thing I knew, I was standing here.

Not, to my surprise, on a grassy field at Gettysburg as planned, but in a strange, unearthly place. I'll attempt to describe what I'm seeing.

Before me, a long corridor stretches out as far as the eye can see, all the way to infinity. It consists of a series of rings, each approximately twenty feet in diameter. The inner surface of the rings — I'm standing on one now — is made of some translucent material which emits a soft, white light.

I'm reaching down and touching the surface, which is amazingly smooth. My fingers glide across it with no sense of friction. Could these rings be made not of physical matter but of some form of solid light? I don't think that's possible, but perhaps the standard laws of physics don't apply here. Turning around, I notice that the corridor extends behind me in the other direction, also with no end in sight.

The rings do not form one continuous conduit but are broken up into segments about ten feet wide. Between the rings there are gaps which appear to be open to outer space. How can I be breathing? But I am, so it's either an illusion or some perfectly clear material. I'm stepping out onto this break in the rings — and I'm standing on empty space. The view is amazing! So many stars. But no close suns or planets. I don't recognize any constellations.

Something's happening. Down the corridor, it's beginning to get darker. In the distance the rings of light are vanishing one by one. Even the stars beyond them are disappearing. Behind me, the corridor is collapsing too.

From both sides, a wall of darkness is rapidly closing in on me. The effect creates the sensation of movement as if I'm falling toward the end of the tunnel, either way I look.

My heart races as I watch, mesmerized by forces I can't begin to understand. I fear this may be my first and final log entry. I …

———

… find myself standing on green grass in a wide-open field. Bright blue sky above with a hawk gliding in circles, catching the breeze. In the distance, trees show off their fallcolors. Could this be Gettysburg? It must be. I made it! Unbelievable!

But what happened moments ago? Where was I? Perhaps that corridor was some kind of portal or nexus connecting all points of spacetime. Did an advanced race of beings build it, or has it always existed as part of the structure of the universe? We may never know. I'll simply refer to it as the Corridor with a capital C.

Now to the mission at hand. I'll try to keep my descriptions as objective as possible, but that will be difficult, I admit. Jumping two centuries back in time to witness one of the most famous events in American history is anything but impersonal, especially for a historian.

Currently, I'm standing about two hundred yards from a large crowd gathering around the speakers' stand. This plot of ground is close to where Robert E. Lee ordered his final assault on the Union position on the hill before being forced to retreat. John Rey and Rosa's calculations were quite accurate. We chose this spot far enough away from today's activities so that no one would witness me materializing out of thin air.

I glance down at my attire: a standard military uniform of the Union Army, a dark-blue wool coat with brass buttons down the front. The insignia on the sleeves indicates a rank of corporal. The cuffs are frayed from wear. The light blue pants have stains on the knees.

The illusion is perfect. The chamo-suit functions like the techs said it would. They named it after the chameleon since it changes appearance as needed. The surface of the suit consists of microscopic nano-projectors which emit pixels of light to create a convincing image to the eye as long as no one touches it. I am not supposed to interact physically with others anyway, so hopefully that won't be a problem.

Much of the science behind the suit escapes me; all I know is that it works. No time traveler should leave home without one. It's strange wearing a rough wool outfit that doesn't feel hot or scratchy. I assume the suit's hood is projecting the image of a blue cap on my head, and I'm tempted to reach up and touch it, but I realize I wouldn't feel anything there. Hopefully, I'll find a mirror somewhere or at least a pool of water to view my reflection.

I'm climbing the hill approaching the speakers' platform. The ravaged ground shows evidence of the shallow graves hastily dug after the battle. I try not to step on them, but there are so many. Some have temporary wooden markers identifying the individual; many others do not.

As I make my way toward the crowd, which contemporary reports estimated at twenty thousand, the noise level is surprisingly low. The people are speaking to one another in hushed tones. There's no shouting or laughter. The solemnity of this site has affected everyone here.

On such a beautiful sunny day, it's hard to imagine the carnage that took place here a few months ago. In contrast to the present tranquility, those three days in July were filled with the thundering of cannons and the horrible cries of dying men in the bloodiest battle of the Civil War. Over seven thousand were killed in action or died of their wounds and disease in the days following. To commemorate the fallen, the governor of Pennsylvania decided to establish the Soldier's National Cemetery on this battleground.

My arrival time is perfect. Standing at the edge of the crowd, I can see the president now, riding a chestnut horse with others in procession. Lincoln is dressed in black, wearing a dark crepe band around his stovepipe hat, a sign of mourning for his young son Willie who died of typhoid fever the previous year. The president receives a military salute as he and members of his cabinet occupy the platform with other dignitaries. Many men in the crowd uncover their heads in respect, although some near me grumble to one another, complaining about his mishandling of the war and the issue of slavery. I want to speak up in his defense but dare not.

A photographer is setting up his camera on a tripod. It must be Matthew Brady, whose work will preserve this important period in American history. His haunting images of fields littered with bodies made this war a vivid reality to the people back home. Perhaps I can meet him after the speeches. Surely a simple handshake won't trigger a time paradox.

There's a sense of anticipation in the air, awaiting the arrival of the featured speaker Edward Everett. In his day Everett, a former governor and senator, was regarded as one of the country's finest orators, and most of the crowd have come today to hear him, not the president.

Initially, the organizers had not included Lincoln in the ceremony, but when he responded to the formal invitation sent to all important public figures, they had no choice but to schedule him on the program, requesting he make "a few appropriate remarks." Would anyone now remember this day if they hadn't?

Following a prayer and music by the Marine Band, Everett begins his speech. From history I know it will go on for almost two hours. His eloquent phrases seem to please the audience, but they strike me as flowery, pompous, and too eager to impress with his comparisons to ancient Greek battles and quotations from the classics.

That's not why I'm here. I watch Lincoln, captivated by his stately presence, his smallest gestures, his facial expressions, his stifled yawn while Everett drones on. One time he takes his glasses from his coat pocket and reviews his handwritten notes.

I also observe the men around me with their tired, hardened faces weary of this war. It has taken its toll on soldiers and civilians alike. Some men have nodded to me with respect for my apparent service while others view my uniform with sadness, perhaps seeing a reminder of someone they have lost.

Finally, the agonizing wait is over. Lincoln walks to the podium. He takes a moment to look over the audience and clears his throat. He holds his manuscript in front of him but does not read from it. He begins: "Four score and seven years ago, our fathers brought forth on this continent a new nation ..."

There's no need to record the rest of these immortal words, spoken in less than three minutes. But I can't truly describe the feeling of hearing them from the mouth of the one who wrote them. The familiar phrases sound so fresh and alive, filled with significance. Surely these men standing here can sense that these words will outlast them.

But contemporary reports tell a different story. At the time, many people considered the speech unexceptional. Lincoln himself told a companion that his address was a failure and had disappointed the people. Even in the address, he said, "The world will little note nor long remember what we say here." How wrong he was. I wish I could tell him.

The ceremony concludes, and the crowd disperses, but I am still standing here, dazzled by what I have witnessed. Although in my academic career I specialized in studying ancient civilizations, I have always found this period of American history fascinating. I admire Lincoln immensely and find myself contemplating a tempting possibility.

What if I return a few months before April 15, 1865? I could search for John Wilkes Booth; as a famous actor, he was a public figure and not difficult to find. Could I stop him somehow? Could I save the life of this man whose words have moved me so?

But I know this is impossible. Our Chronos team has had many late-night discussions about the potential dangers of tinkering with time, opening up too many unforeseeable consequences. Changing the past could alter the present for better or much, much worse. No one has the right to make such decisions affecting the lives of billions.

My stomach is growling, reminding me of how long it's been since I've eaten. Perhaps I can locate a pub in the town before I'm transported back to the present. I'm assuming I bought a round-trip ticket. As much as I've enjoyed my visit, I don't feel like making 1863 my home; I appreciate antibiotics, movies, and indoor plumbing too much. I trust that if my team of experts got me here, they can return me to where I belong.

This is Martin Chamberlain, signing off.

///end log///

3

August 8, 2059

ONCE THE LOG TRANSCRIPT CONCLUDED, THE TEAM SAT FOR a few moments until David broke the silence with "Wow." The reality that they had actually sent a man through time and brought him back safely impressed even the "wise-crack wizard," as the others called him. David was fond of the title.

"Remarkable. Truly remarkable." S.P. patted him on the back. "Martin, you handled yourself admirably on this first mission."

"All the data checks out so far," Rosa added, reviewing the computer screens. "We'll need to compare everything to our theoretical models, but right now, I'm very pleased — and excited. Like David said, 'Wow.'"

Andrea spoke up. "John Rey and Rosa, once you have confirmed the information and are certain the log reflects what truly happened, I'll deliver the official report to our sponsor. But Martin, I must say: you were in the pod for twelve hours. We never opened the lid during that time, so none of us saw your disappearing act. How do we know that you didn't take a long nap and dream all of this?"

The others stared at her.

Undaunted, she pressed on. "With your prior knowledge of the event, coupled with a vivid imagination, you could have invented all the details of this wild story. Pardon my skepticism, but I represent the sponsor's interests and significant investment in this project. I have to ask the hard questions if no one else will."

"That's OK," Martin responded. "No offense taken. But if you want some evidence, follow me to my office."

He led Andrea and the others down the hall. From his bookcase filled with history texts, he selected a volume titled *America's Greatest Conflict*. "One of my professors in grad school wrote this. It's fully illustrated. Turn to the page with the bookmark."

Andrea flipped through the book and examined the old photograph reproduced there.

"Matthew Brady took that photo on the day of the Gettysburg Address," Martin explained. "Look over to the right side of this grouping of men. There, in the back." Andrea squinted at the image, then her eyes widened. "Yes, that's me."

David grabbed the book from her while John Rey and Rosa peeked over his shoulder to see the photo.

Martin smiled. "I wanted a souvenir of the trip and assumed this one change wouldn't have any serious historical consequences."

Andrea had to admit, "This does seem convincing."

"And I swear, that photo didn't have me in it yesterday."

S.P. chuckled. "I think he's got you, my dear."

"Well, I'll accept this evidence for what it appears to be, for now. John Rey, when will you have your report ready?"

"Rosa and I should be able to get it done by tomorrow. After that, we'll start on the recalibrations for the next jump with David's assistance."

"And remind me, when is that scheduled?" S.P. asked. "I need to make a quick trip to Santa Fe for supplies. Will there be time?"

"Odd question to ask someone with a time machine," David quipped.

"We are aiming for one week from today as long as the diagnostic tests of the equipment go smoothly," Rosa replied with John Rey nodding in agreement.

"Where to next, Martin?" S.P. never paid attention at the planning meetings.

"May 6, 1937. The Hindenburg airship disaster."

"Very well," said Andrea. "I suppose you have the week off, Martin. Enjoy yourself. Dr. Hewes, have a safe trip. Be sure to turn in your expense report. We'll see everyone back together here in seven days."

During the next week, Martin struggled to find activities that would interest him. Reading the history books that filled every room of his home paled in comparison to his thrilling experience at Gettysburg. He couldn't get the sights, sounds, and smells of the past out of his head. He thought about rewatching classic films by his favorite twentieth century directors like Alfred Hitchcock and Steven Spielberg, but he wasn't in the mood for second-hand adventures.

So instead of his usual pastimes, he spent most of his days walking the neighborhoods of Roswell with his dog Sadie. But there are times when an affectionate golden retriever cannot take the place of more desirable companionship.

After a few days, he worked up the courage to break the ice and announced to his house system, "Contact Andrea Carlton." The seconds ticked by like hours as he anxiously waited for a response. His heart raced; his palms felt clammy. Defending his dissertation before the graduate committee had been a breeze compared to asking a woman out — in particular, this woman.

Then the comm screen, which filled one wall of his home office, lit up. It looked as if Andrea were standing in an adjacent room.

"Hello, Martin. What a surprise."

"Andrea. How are you?"

"I'm fine, thank you. Can I help you with something?"

"Oh, I was wondering if … This may seem rather abrupt, but I want to ask … Well, we see each other at the Chronos center, but I really don't know you that well. Would you perhaps …"

"Martin, if you are asking me for a date, I'm rather busy."

"Not a date, really. That is, we don't have to call it that. Nothing serious. It's just that I've wanted to take a tour of the Snowy River Cave in Fort Stanton and wondered if you might be interested in going along. Think of it as historical research of the Paleozoic era." He chuckled lamely.

"Martin, I firmly believe professional relationships should remain professional."

"Yes, I agree … in theory, but …"

"Now if you will excuse me, there's a lot still to do before the next jump."

"All right, I guess I'll see you —" but she had already exited the call.

When it came to reading women, Martin had to admit he was practically illiterate.

"Well, Sadie, it looks like it's just you and me, girl. How about another walk?" Sadie was one step ahead of him, bringing her leash in her mouth. She never turned down a date.

The town of Roswell was an isolated oasis in the desert of southeastern New Mexico. Its population had remained stable for many decades, having grown a bit to around seventy thousand after the eastern migration following the Great California Quake in '45. In a world of nine billion people, Martin appreciated that some places still retained their small town charm. He was glad that the Chronos Project had located about twenty miles outside the city limits. He certainly did not miss his apartment on the 285th floor of the Metroplex skyscraper in Chicago with its twelve thousand residents. Sadie liked it better here too.

Roswell's biggest claim to fame was the International UFO Museum and Research Center. The alleged UFO incident in 1947 was named after the town, although the crash site had occurred about seventy-five miles away. Men at the Roswell Army Air Field had handled the investigation and debris recovery of what official reports described as a downed weather balloon. The town continued to attract curious sightseers seeking evidence of extraterrestrial visitations.

Martin stayed away from the tourist traps, preferring to stroll with Sadie through the peace and quiet of his charming residential neighborhood — that is, until the quietness was broken by the illuminated floating billboards which followed him everywhere. By linking to his cyber-chip and retrieving his personal data, the small screens offered him special deals on food, merchandise, travel packages, romantic diversions, and anything else tailored to his interests.

"Look at this one, Sadie? What do you think?" The screen hovering a few feet above his head depicted happy people enjoying their "round-the-world" cruise on the luxurious Heavenly Holiday space station where "your earthly troubles float away." In one scene, a man and woman were playing a zero-gravity version of dodgeball, attempting to anticipate the ball's direction as it bounced off the twenty slanted walls of the chamber. A young boy and girl giggled as they squirted juice bottles and tried to swallow the quivering globules.

"You think you'd like weightlessness, Sadie?" She responded with a very negative-sounding growl.

No sooner had he dismissed the vacation ad than another popped into view. "Virtual Vision places you right at the scene of the action. Dr. Chamberlain, we recommend our Civil War reenactment package with all the excitement and none of the danger. Don't merely read about history. Experience it!" Martin had to laugh at that one. Sadie barked again.

Tiring of the intrusions, he mentally signaled his chip to refuse commercials for now and asked for some Mozart. A favorite, "Piano Concerto No. 21," began playing in his head. He walked with a quicker step to the music, which made Sadie happy. They continued down the sidewalk past modest residences with their rooftop solar panels gleaming in the afternoon sunlight. The air was so much fresher since the country had finally adopted the widespread use of renewable energy sources over the objection of some politicians and their Big Oil contributors.

Automatic electric cars purred by them, their occupants reading or sleeping. Martin casually wondered where they were going. Certainly not anywhere as exciting as he would be in a few days. He felt grateful for this amazing opportunity, recollecting how he had first learned of the Chronos Project.

4

Eleven months earlier

For nine years after earning his PhD from Princeton, Martin had taught in the department of history at the University of Chicago. He enjoyed his courses and interacting with his graduate students, but he missed research. His department encouraged scholarly publication, but he didn't want to spend more time reading books and articles. He wanted field work, getting his hands dirty at an archaeological site or discovering some forgotten manuscript misfiled in an old library archive.

So when he saw the notice on his computer screen for "a unique opportunity to conduct original, firsthand research" along with the qualification "only for the adventurous," he applied for an interview. What did he have to lose?

Admittedly, most people would not consider this tenured professor as the adventurous type, but secretly

Martin pictured himself as another Indiana Jones with an imposing name like Sahara Sam or Dirk Deadly. He had recurring dreams of exploring tropical jungles in search of crumbling temples hiding lost treasures, or diving deep into the ocean to discover sunken Atlantis. The other night, his imagination had transported him to ancient Egypt where he had confronted a living sphinx protecting the Great Pyramid.

Waking up from his thrilling fantasies, he was always a bit disappointed to return to reality. Maybe this new job would offer a unique challenge or two to spice up his humdrum routine.

The next morning, he received a response from the source of the email, inviting him to fly to Roswell, New Mexico, all expenses paid. Immediately he cancelled his afternoon class, giving them an online assignment, and scheduled a first-class flight.

Once he arrived, an automated limousine picked him up at the airport and drove to the private medical facility where the interview would be conducted. The email had indicated that there would be physical and psychological exams as part of the process. Martin appeared to be the only visitor at the facility this day; there was one other car in the lot, parked in a space reserved for staff.

The man who greeted him at the door introduced himself as Dr. Hewes and invited Martin into a side room. After a standard medical exam with the usual blood work, Martin took a physical endurance test to check his heart and stamina. Then he sat for two hours at a computer screen answering hundreds of questions about world history, foreign languages, and fluency with various

American and English dialects. The program wrapped up with personality tests to determine his ability to adapt to new situations, and oddly enough, any problems with claustrophobia.

When the tests concluded, Dr. Hewes entered the room. With no comments on how he had done, the doctor ushered him out to the limousine again that drove about twenty miles outside Roswell to an isolated location off US Highway 380. Pulling up to the site, Martin felt somewhat apprehensive, seeing a one-story building with an unimpressive exterior and no signage. *This company certainly wants to stay unnoticed.* Miles of empty desert stretched out in all directions.

A man answered the door. Without introducing himself or asking Martin's identity, he directed him through a small lobby to a hallway with closed doors at both ends. Martin sat on a cushioned bench, wondering what he had gotten himself into.

He glanced at the picture on the wall in front of him, a quality reproduction of Salvador Dali's *The Persistence of Memory* with its surrealistic depiction of melting clocks. Then he observed that behind him was an original work by a contemporary artist. He stood to examine it more closely.

In it, an elderly woman in a wheelchair held a portrait of herself as a smartly dressed woman in her forties, who in turn was holding a portrait of herself as a wistful teenager longing to be an adult, who was holding one of herself as a little girl peering into a cradle. All but the young girl were gazing directly at the viewer in an unnerving fashion. Martin then noticed a final, haunting detail. At the edges of the painting, skeletal fingers grasped the canvas as if the woman were viewing the receding images of her life from beyond the grave.

In a way the painting reminded him of his visit a few years ago to a little church in Rome, Santa Maria della Concezione dei Cappuccini. During the Renaissance, the church's crypt had been elaborately decorated with the bones of thousands of friars. A motto on the wall read: "What you are now, we once were. What we are now, you shall be." The recollection sent chills up his spine.

Underneath the painting was a small metal plaque that noted the work had been commissioned by the sponsor of the project. Martin reflected on the patron's macabre taste in art and wondered who he or she might be.

"Martin Chamberlain, please come with me." The woman's voice startled him as he hadn't heard anyone enter the hall. She wore a dark-blue suit with a simple string of pearls. With glasses and hair pulled into a bun, she gave the impression of a government official, all business, no humor. Martin guessed she was in her mid-thirties. He followed her to an expensively furnished office.

After they both sat down, she introduced herself. "My name is Andrea Carlton. I represent the founder and underwriter of the Chronos Project. I will explain the nature of our work shortly. But first, congratulations. You have been accepted as part of the team."

Martin paused, taken aback by the swiftness of the entire process. "I must say I'm pleased. Thank you. But what about the other candidates? Don't you need time to notify —"

"There are no other candidates. You were the only one who was invited. We investigated you thoroughly before sending the initial notice to your computer, which no one else received. Our sponsor wanted you, and I saw to it. So the only decision left is for you to accept the offer."

Martin didn't know how to respond. This woman was impressive, not so much for her appearance but for her demeanor as a person certain of what she wanted and confident she could get it. Apparently, at the moment, she wanted him in this position, whatever that might be.

"I'm sorry, but I'm not sure of what this — 'Chronos Project,' did you call it? — what this project is about. And why all the secrecy, way out here in the middle of nowhere? It's unnerving, to say the least. I need more information before committing to anything."

"The founder of our enterprise, who prefers to remain anonymous, has resources considerable enough to fund all of our research without financial associates or supervising boards. The nature of the project requires a high level of security; thus we try to draw as little attention to our work as possible."

After sipping from a glass of water, she continued. "Several years ago, our sponsor had a revolutionary idea and conceived of a way theoretically to travel through time." She paused while Martin processed this surprising information. "With an expert team carefully chosen for their achievements in various fields, we have worked tirelessly for the last few years and now are close to achieving success, turning theory into reality."

Seeing the incredulity in his face, Andrea held up her hand to stop him from interrupting. "Now you understand why we must keep the nature of our project a secret. If the world knew about this ability, many people would attempt to exploit it for selfish and malevolent purposes. Political leaders could use the technology to eliminate their rivals before they were born. Governments could launch preemptive strikes in the past against enemy nations. Religious fanatics might try to assassinate the founders of rival faiths. Not to mention the potential uses for organized crime. In contrast, the mission of the Chronos Project will be pure research of historical events with as little interference as possible. We seek to learn from the past, not alter it."

Martin wondered if he had stepped into the Twilight Zone. As a student of history, he had often wished for a time machine to explore significant events of the past, but he knew this idea was mere fantasy, the stuff of Hollywood movies. Did this woman take him for a fool? Before he could voice any objections, however, Andrea stood and led him to another room, dark except for one spotlight illuminating a beautiful Greek vase on a pedestal.

"Examine it if you wish. You'll find it to be in pristine condition."

He walked closer to the display. "Yes, it's truly a remarkable find. This depiction of Achilles before the battle was a popular subject for classical amphorae. I assume there's been some restoration? Surely you didn't recover it in such perfect shape."

"No restoration or recovery. The vase is new. Fresh from the hand of the craftsman who created it. Notice his name around the base."

Martin looked more closely. "Exekias. Yes, I recognize the style now. He was one of the first Greek artisans to sign his work. But you aren't suggesting … no, that's impossible. Exekias lived in the sixth century BC."

"The time from which we retrieved the vase."

He stepped back, startled. "You mean someone has actually traveled through time?"

"Not a living subject, no. At the current stage, the process only allowed us to snatch this single object from the past as a test. We are a few months away from human trials."

"And, I'm guessing, that you want a historian as your guinea pig?" He still had strong doubts about this project, and his raised eyebrows showed it.

"No need for concern. We are extremely confident in our R&D team. They will achieve the objective. The only question here is if you choose to be part of this, shall we say, historic event?"

5

August 15, 2059

"So, Martin, are you ready to do this?"

Andrea's question brought him out of his contemplation of how he had arrived at the present moment. He'd gone over the sequence of events in his mind several times over the last few days, appreciating how fortunate he was that they had selected him for this opportunity.

The Chronos Project would allow historians to investigate firsthand some mysteries about the past which remained unanswered: Who was Jack the Ripper? What happened to the Ark of the Covenant? Was there a second gunshot from the grassy knoll in Dealey Plaza? Soon others would get a crack at solving these enigmas, but for now, Martin was the star of the show.

During the last week, John Rey, Rosa, and David had double-checked the results from the first human test run and determined they were all set for another trip. Still uncertain about the scientific principles behind the process, Martin had asked them how they could pinpoint the precise location of the jump along with the correct date.

Rosa's response: "Once you master time travel, space travel is easy."

He took that as another way of saying, "You wouldn't understand it, anyway. Stick to history."

Dr. Hewes had concluded his physical examination a few minutes ago and pronounced Martin fit for the journey. Dressed in his chamo-suit, Martin stood beside the pod that momentarily would transfer him, if all went as planned, to Manchester Township, New Jersey, 1937, the site of the Hindenburg disaster. He took a final survey of the room.

He admired this team. They were smart and dedicated and had achieved the impossible. They hadn't done it alone. In total, about sixty experts from different fields had brought the Chronos Project to fruition, but the others had worked in isolated groups in several places around the country, unaware of the goal of their combined efforts. Only the six people in this room and their mysterious sponsor knew the true nature of the project.

With a final wave to everyone, he settled into the watery solution in the pod and tried to relax. For some reason, Andrea had decided that she wanted the honor this time of closing the lid. "Pleasant dreams, Martin."

"I promise to stay awake, thinking of you."

"Nice try." She sealed the pod shut.

In the darkness, the sensation of floating began to make him feel drowsy.

<hr>

Once again, Martin found himself standing in the mysterious Corridor, its glowing rings extending out to infinity. But this time — something was different. Something was wrong.

He was not alone.

6

August 16, 2059

"RISE AND SHINE, MARTIN. YOU'RE BACK."

Slowly, he sat up in the pod and shook his head. The dense fog in his mind wouldn't clear. Something had just happened — but what?

"John Rey, what's the status?" Andrea asked, always expecting immediate results.

"Good so far. Sensors say the distortion wave has leveled out as predicted. I think we can mark this as another successful round trip through time."

"Martin, how do you feel? Any different this time?" S.P. reached out and took his pulse. "Frankly, you look a bit pale."

Eager for another exciting report, Rosa inquired, "What do you remember?"

"Give him a minute," John Rey cautioned her. "He's still coming out of it. Besides, we have the log to review."

Rosa helped him out of the pod and gave him a towel

to dry off. He glanced around the room at the team, who all seemed familiar — but different as well. Something about their clothing, their hairstyles, what? A glint in the light caught his eye.

"Andrea, you're wearing a ring. When did that happen?"

"Martin, he proposed six months ago. What's the matter with you? Are you all right?"

"I'm not sure. Something feels … off."

S.P. intervened on his patient's behalf. "I recommend we let him rest a while. His pulse does read a bit high. Perhaps we can delay the log download until tomorrow."

"But I want to know what happened to the Hindenburg," Rosa whined.

"It blew up. End of story." David summed it up nicely.

"I mean, I want Martin's perspective on it. What was it like being right there? I'm sorry, but I'm impatient."

David responded, "What's the rush? With what we've got here in this room, we truly have all the time in the world."

"I agree," Andrea said. "Let's give Martin a day to rest and recover. Seeing this disaster in person has apparently shaken him up."

"Oh, the humanity!"

"David, that's very insensitive, even for you. Just for that, you see that he gets home. We'll convene here tomorrow morning to review the log."

Grateful for the reprieve, Martin allowed David to help him to the company car (*was it green before?*) where he climbed into the passenger seat. Surprised, he watched as David slid behind the wheel on the driver's side.

"What are you doing?"

"What does it look like I'm doing? I'm taking you home. You think these things drive themselves?"

Too exhausted to argue, he leaned back in the seat and instantly fell asleep. A few minutes later, his nap was cut short by the sound of a car racing by, spewing a trail of smoke.

"Hey, buddy, get a tune-up! The garage is that way, idiot," David yelled, pointing the other driver in the appropriate direction with a helpful gesture.

Martin didn't remember when he had last seen a gas-powered car, but then they passed another one in the opposite lane, not fuming but, obviously by its sound, with an internal combustion engine.

Soon, David pulled up to Martin's apartment complex. The location was not the best with the towers of the Roswell nuclear reactor looming in the distance, but the rent was reasonable. Martin thanked David for the lift and wearily stumbled to his door, where Sadie eagerly awaited him.

"Hey, girl. Yes, I've missed you too. Did Mrs. Starnes feed you and let you out while I was gone?" Sadie barked. The place seemed clean, so he assumed she had. "I'm really tired, but I suppose you want to take a walk. Maybe a short one around the block. Where's your leash?"

Sadie sat and looked at him, wagging her tail. "Go on, girl, you know where it is. Get your leash." Sadie cocked her head to one side and whined, a bit confused at her master's request. "OK, this is crazy. An engagement ring, gas-powered cars, and now this? Will someone tell me what's going on?"

The time jump; that must be it. Something happened, something very bad.

He struggled to recall what had occurred, but nothing came to him except an ominous sense that this was just the beginning. But of what? He would have to wait until tomorrow's review of his log. A long, sleepless night lay ahead of him.

7

Chronos Project
Personal Mission Log: Dr. Martin Chamberlain
Departure date: August 15, 2059
Target destination: Manchester Township, New Jersey
Target date: May 6, 1937

THIS IS MARTIN CHAMBERLAIN REPORTING ON MY SECOND trip through time. I have materialized in the spacetime Corridor again — and realize I'm not alone. Someone or something is standing about twenty feet away from me.

The creature has a large head, vaguely reptilian in shape, with a protruding jaw filled with razor-sharp teeth. Two curved horns sprout from above its solid black eyes. Its skin is a greenish gray and rough, perhaps scaly if I could get a closer look. Surrounding its neck like a lion's mane are pointed, leafy projections seemingly made of bone and blood-red in color.

Beneath this gruesome head, its body resembles a barbell, a cylindrical waist with muscular bulges above and below. From each of these bulges, three appendages radiate at equal distance, thus surrounding the creature with three arms and three legs. On its back an undulating sac expands and contracts. This might be a heart or lungs, but given the unearthly nature of the alien, I can only guess what its function is.

Yes, I can't deny it. As incredible as it sounds, that's what this is: a genuine, out of this world, I-can't-believe-I'm-seeing-this ALIEN. An interstellar being from another planet or galaxy or far-distant future. Anything is possible.

The alien is turning. He sees me, but he's not approaching. He's moving his head up and down as if nodding at me. Should I respond? Now he's gesturing with something in one of his hands. A metallic device — perhaps a weapon?

Wait a minute. Behind the alien, the rings of light are vanishing like they did before. Down the Corridor, the darkness rushes toward us in total silence. Will it transport us together into the past? What if …?

The alien has vanished, but I'm still here in the Corridor, which once again extends to infinity. The transference worked for him. Why not me?

"Hello, Martin."

I turn and notice another figure in the Corridor behind me. This one looks human, an older man with gray hair and a pleasant, non-threatening smile. He reminds me of my grandfather, gone now for many years.

"Yes, I've taken on a shape familiar to you, hoping you will accept my presence more readily. In reality, this form you see is only a mental projection. That's why you can understand what I say."

"Who are you?"

"A friend. Someone who wants to help. And right now, you need help."

I can't argue with that. "What was that creature who was here before?"

"You could not pronounce his name if you tried. Let's refer to him as the Other."

"And you? Do you have a name?"

"Our people do not have names. We all know who we are."

This is all too strange, even stranger than hearing a dead president speak. Am I losing my mind? "This Other. What can you tell me about him?"

"First, I refer to the Other as 'he,' but in truth, neither his race nor mine has two sexes as humans do. The Other belongs to a species whose homeworld is far from your sun. They are one of a few galactic societies who have mastered the technique of temporal transit. The Others discovered the Corridor about the same time as my people did. A long time ago. Now your species has joined this illustrious community."

"Did you create the Corridor?"

"Oh, no. Its origins are a mystery. Lost in time, as it were."

"This is unreal. Just when I was getting used to traveling into the past, I meet ... you. And this alien. You said I need help. Am I in danger?"

"The scope of the danger encompasses more than one person. Let me explain. My people respect Time. We admire the beauty of its flow and wish not to disturb the intricate designs it creates. Some races like the Others do not share our philosophy. With no regard for the purity of Time, they choose to tamper with the histories of other worlds. Now this one has chosen yours."

"Can you stop him?"

"My people follow a strict code. We disapprove of what the Others are doing, but we cannot interfere with another race's reality, even to preserve it. We must leave this task up to you."

"Why me?"

"At this point in your history, you are your world's only Traveler."

"What must I do? How can I stop him?"

"Go back to your present world. You will notice some things have changed. Only you, however, will recognize these alterations since only you have stepped outside the stream of time during the shift. Your investigations should lead you to the critical juncture when the Other disrupted your timeline. You must return to that time in your history and repair the damage."

"You mean, interfere with time again. That's the problem. I joined this project to research the past, not to change it."

"That's very wise. But unfortunately, others do not share your respect for the way things are. They view time as a medium to manipulate."

"Like a potter molding clay."

"Precisely. I said I cannot help you directly, but when you return, you will find that I have made some modifications to the device you wear inside your head."

"My cyber-chip? What will it do?"

"I leave that for you to discover. I must send you back now. Best wishes or Godspeed or good luck, I believe your people may say at the occasion of departure."

///end log///

8

August 17, 2059

"Wow."

"You said that last time, David."

"Yeah, but this time I really mean it. Just … wow."

The team stared at one another in astonishment, attempting to process what they had read on the screen. For Martin, the odd things he had observed since returning were beginning to make sense. Somehow this was no longer his reality.

Finally, John Rey spoke up. "How about that? We actually did find an alien in Roswell."

"First time travel *and* first contact. I'm certain this qualifies you for a Guinness World Record," Rosa added with a broad smile.

"A historian making history." S.P. was clearly impressed.

Martin's colleagues thought his story was strange but

credible. Andrea, however, remained suspicious. "Are you sure you didn't imagine all this? It sounds delusional."

"I don't know what to believe," Martin admitted. "Now that I've reviewed the log, the memories have come back crystal clear. It seemed real at the time, but …"

"What should we call these aliens?" John Rey asked.

"I say the first one with all the limbs should be Xenox. X-e-n-o-x." David was the resident sci-fi and fantasy geek.

"Why Xenox?"

"It sounds cool."

S.P. remarked, "Actually, that's rather appropriate since it's based on the Greek root word we use for a foreigner or other, as in the term 'xenophobia.'"

"What about the second guy?"

"I like to regard him as our ally," Martin said, and the name stuck.

David took control of the conversation. "All right, assuming that this Ally is on the level —"

"That's a questionable assumption, I point out."

"Oh, lighten up, Andrea. All my life I've known we were not alone in the universe. Martin's report sounds perfectly logical to me. Why would he make this stuff up? Besides, he doesn't have the imagination."

"I remind all of you that I must run this by our sponsor."

"You do that, Andrea. Meanwhile, we'll be concentrating on saving the world."

"If I may," S.P. interjected. "I'm not an expert in these matters, but if the Ally is correct that this Xenox will interfere with our history, or perhaps already has, then how would we recognize that? We are part of that history."

"S.P.'s right," John Rey added. "Martin's the only one who hasn't been floating down the river of time with us, you might say."

"That's what the Ally suggested. I'm supposed to identify changes in our society or in world history at large. It's a formidable task."

"Have you noticed anything thus far?" Andrea asked.

"I'd rather not get into that yet." Martin thought about her ring, wondering who the lucky guy was. "Not until I have time to consider it. I'm having some trouble sorting out what I remember that *was* and what I'm seeing that *is*. Past and present are overlapping."

"Why don't you start gathering information," Rosa suggested. "Any clues that our world's timeline may have changed. Write them down so you don't forget. Then perhaps we can help investigate those things to find any correlations."

"Very well," Andrea agreed. "Under the circumstances, we should postpone our next expedition into the past until we better understand what's happening. Martin, you are free to explore the possibilities all you want. For the rest of you, I'll need to hear what our sponsor decides about all this before authorizing any additional research by the team."

Andrea went to her office to submit her report. Dr. Hewes gathered up his medical equipment and put it away. David returned to his computer, pretending to work on a program while actually playing a game. John

Rey and Rosa withdrew to a corner and spoke to one another in their traditional Filipino language.

<<Can you believe it? This is so wild! How can we know what's real and what's not?>>

<<Yes, it's crazy. What if we find out that we were lovers in the previous reality, or even married?>>

<<In your dreams, John Rey, in your dreams.>>

"Actually," Martin interrupted, "I don't recall any matrimonial plans for you two."

"What was that, Martin?" Rosa looked embarrassed. "I didn't know you understood Tagalog."

"I … I don't," he admitted. "I guess I picked up a few phrases being around you guys."

Troubled by what just happened, he made a swift exit and headed home. He had much to contemplate.

Later that afternoon, Martin consulted with his trusted advisor about the extraordinary situation he found himself in.

"Sadie, old girl, I need to talk, and you need a walk."

Grabbing her leash, they left the apartment, then headed down the sidewalk. He noticed the cars driving by were noisier, and the air didn't smell as clean and fresh as before. He entertained the idea that Xenox was in league with the oil industry but dismissed it as unlikely.

"It's strange, Sadie. Well, all of it's strange, but right now I'm remembering that conversation I overheard with Rosa and John Rey. I'm sure they were speaking in

Tagalog, which they often do together, but I swear I heard it in English."

Sadie barked. She seemed to enjoy these conversations.

"The odd thing is that I saw their lips moving, but the words I heard didn't match what I saw. It's almost as if the voices were coming from inside my head."

<<That is correct.>>

"What?" Martin looked around for one of the ubiquitous floating billboards but saw nothing. He stopped. Sadie tugged on the leash, but her master was lost in thought. "There's no one here. Am I losing it? Has something about these temporal jumps damaged my mind?"

<<No physical injury occurred due to my insertion.>>

"Who said that?" He turned in all directions, but other than Sadie, he was alone. "Where are you? Wait — is this the Ally?"

<<Negative, but the one designated 'Ally' is responsible for the modification.>>

"What modi … oh, of course. He said he would modify my chip in some way. That must be it. So, you *are* in my head."

<<Correct.>>

"Are you an AI?"

<<If by that classification you mean an artificial intelligence, yes. I have been incorporated into your cybernetic implant.>>

Martin laughed. "That's great! At least, I hope so. What can you do? He implied you could assist me."

<<My primary function concerns translation.>>

"So you caused me to hear John Rey and Rosa in English? That's fantastic! I mean, we've had translating programs for several decades, but not like this. Instantaneous translation in my mind."

He became excited considering the ramifications. "Yes, that's precisely what I may need if I have to journey to another country or an ancient civilization. So far, we were limiting our research jumps to recent history in America or other English-speaking cultures. Say, will I be able to communicate in other languages as well?"

<<Yes. The cybernetic device links to the speech centers of your brain.>>

Sadie tugged again on her leash.

"I'm sorry, girl. I'm neglecting you, aren't I? But I'm feeling better now that I understand what's happened. Come on, let's keep going." They continued down the street. "So what else can you do? Can you help me solve this massive puzzle I've been given? Can you tell me what changes have occurred in our timeline, if anything?"

<<At present, my primary function concerns translation.>>

"Yes, you said that. But what do you mean 'at present'? Is that liable to change?"

<<Correct. I am currently performing self-diagnostic calibrations to determine the possibility of future modifications.>>

"OK, so far so good. After all this is over, if it's ever over, maybe you can help me win at black jack."

<<I do not understand. Explain 'black jack.'>>

"Never mind. A bad joke. We've got more important things to do. Sadie, let's go home."

Over the next few weeks, Martin plunged himself into a sea of information, searching for discrepancies in the current timeline from what he remembered. He began with internet news sources, focusing on politics, science and technology, and cultural trends. The AI assisted him in reading foreign websites since the changes could crop up anywhere.

However, he soon realized that most of the differences were relatively insignificant in the larger scheme of world history. America was still consuming fossil fuels. Two presidential candidates in the last forty years had different running mates. The European Union had broken up again. A civil war in Africa had been avoided due to the fall of a corrupt regime. Some good things, some bad things, but nothing out of the ordinary.

He checked further back into the twentieth century. The first moon landing took place in 1971. John F. Kennedy was killed by a car bomb in Dallas. World War II lasted an additional six months. Certain celebrities never achieved fame.

Every few days he shared his findings with the Chronos team who, despite Andrea's skepticism, had received a go-ahead from the sponsor. They searched for some patterns in all the bits of information Martin provided, but at this point they were of little help. None of them had heard of a minor rock-and-roll band from Liverpool named after an insect or the lovely Norma Jeane Mortenson who dreamed of becoming a movie star but died in a car crash after her first film.

Martin turned to reviewing earlier history. He began sorting through the mountainous piles of scholarly books that had filled every room in his place since he moved to Roswell. Organization had never been his strength. Resembling an archaeological dig, his apartment revealed lost treasures discovered under the couch or on top of the fridge.

Once again, the anomalies he found seemed inconsequential and random, pointing in no particular direction as to when the alien might have interfered with the timeline. The American Revolution was ignited by a tax on tobacco rather than tea. In seventeenth century Europe, the Thirty Year's War had lasted twenty years. The reformer Martin Luther had waited until he was sixty to nail his "Twenty-five Theses" to the church door in Hamburg, for which he was burned at the stake the following year.

By the end of the third week of his reading marathon, Martin felt like admitting defeat. Among the hundreds of deviations from what he remembered, nothing stood out as a possible turning point, changing the direction of all that followed.

"Sadie, I could use some help. Any ideas?" He glanced around and didn't see her at first. Then he noticed her lying on the floor beside the bed, reaching with a paw for something. He got down and looked; sure enough, one of her favorite, well-gnawed bones had been hiding there. Using a broom handle, he rescued the old treat and tossed it to her. With a yelp, she scooped it up in her mouth and bounded out of the room, knocking over a stack of books on her way.

Despite the futility of the effort, he started placing the books back in a pile. He noticed one he had forgotten, a history of ancient Rome. Oddly, it felt thicker than he recalled. Thumbing through the first few pages, he studied the table of contents and nearly jumped out of his skin.

"This is it!"

September 9, 2059

"According to the previous timeline, the Roman Republic existed from roughly 500 BC to 27 BC when Caesar Augustus became the first emperor," Martin explained to his colleagues. "The empire, at least the western half, lasted until 476 AD when it fell to the Germanic tribes."

He held up a book as if he were Moses bringing the Ten Commandments down from the mountain. "In contrast, this definitive volume on Roman history says that Rome existed in the form of the Second Republic until 1372, when it didn't fall but was broken up by design into the United Provinces of Greater Italy, which in some form has continued until today." He paused for dramatic effect. "This, my friends, has to be the significant event we've been searching for."

"Are you sure, Martin?" S.P. asked. "I vaguely

remember some of that from high school. Why would Italy's history be so important?"

"Pizza? Spaghetti? Hello?" David quipped. To his chagrin, everyone ignored his attempt at humor.

Martin continued. "Western civilization grew from the roots of ancient Greece and Rome. Our language, our legal system, the political concepts of democracy and republic, our literature, art, and architecture all find their origins in these classical societies. Any change to their history would have enormous impact, like the waves a boulder would make if tossed into a lake. Ironically, this is one reason I didn't see the turning point before. In both timelines, Greek and Roman culture provided the foundation for who we are today. So the overall outline of our history has remained much the same. It's the details that have changed."

In his excitement, Martin began pacing the room as he talked. "The biggest differences occurred in the early years. Rome never fell, so there never was what some have called the Dark Ages in Europe, a long period of political chaos, poverty, disease, and death. Most historians have revised their negative evaluation of that period, but in contrast to the heights of Roman civilization, the name still has some validity, in my opinion. In any case, our current history text mentions none of that. Rome continued to flourish for nine more centuries."

"So if this is truly the case, then what are we concerned about?" John Rey wondered. "If the alien is responsible for our avoiding these Dark Ages, then shouldn't we thank him for it?"

"Hey, I don't want anyone messing around with who we are." David slapped his hand on the desk for emphasis. "It's our planet. If anyone is going to screw things up, it ought to be us doing it."

"And I'm just beginning to understand the ramifications of this alternate timeline," Martin said. "There will surely be many other changes we haven't discovered yet, things that truly matter to the human race."

S.P. spoke up. "I agree. We don't know what this alien wants to accomplish."

David added, "The Ally must have known something bad was going to happen. He went to the trouble of warning us about it. Personally, I trust him."

"But how does this knowledge help us stop Xenox?" Rosa asked. "What did he do to alter the past?"

"That's our next step." Martin pulled out his datapad to write down ideas. "We need to put this period of early Roman history under a microscope and search for anything unusual."

"What, like a myth about a three-armed, three-legged god coming down from Mt. Olympus?" This idea piqued David's interest.

"Might I make a suggestion?" Andrea surprised everyone with her sudden entrance into the discussion. "Shouldn't we review the original log from when Martin met this Xenox? Maybe he left us a clue."

"Like what?"

"Like what he was holding in his hand."

Suddenly, the memory of the alien gesturing with a

metal object in his claw-like hand came rushing back to Martin. "Yes! Why didn't I think of that before? I can see it clearly in my mind."

"Can you describe it? Or better yet, draw a sketch. Then I can do an image search online." David moved over to his work station to open up a program.

Martin closed his eyes to picture the object. "It was a bronze-colored, metallic box, a little over twelve inches in height. There were several gears and levers." He started to draw an intricate design on his pad. "And there was a knob on the side, something like this."

"Say, that's impressive," Rosa noted. "I didn't know you were an artist."

"I drew lots of pictures as a child and thought about studying art. In college during overseas travel courses, instead of keeping a diary, I would sketch images of the places we visited: cathedrals, palaces, famous statues."

"OK, Leonardo. Let me borrow that masterpiece." David took the pad and uploaded the drawing to the visual search engine.

Rosa and John Rey stepped to one side, speaking softly to one another. The AI offered Martin a translation:

<<What do you think of all this?>>

<<I don't know what to believe. It's all happening so fast.>>

<<Yeah. I need some time to process it.>>

<<I need a drink.>>

"Hey, look at this. I got a hit already. Martin, we're onto something." David moved aside to let the others see the image on the monitor.

"What does the description say?" S.P. asked. "I don't have my computer glasses."

David summarized the information for everyone. "It's some kind of early scientific device for calculating eclipses, the movement of planets, phases of the moon, things like that. They speculate it was invented sometime around 100 BC. The interesting thing is that this type of mechanism was centuries ahead of its time. Some describe it as the world's first known analog computer."

"That must be it," Martin concluded. "Introducing such an advanced piece of equipment into early Roman history would have made a significant impact on the development of technology and the sciences. That would have given the Romans the crucial edge over other cultures, improving their already impressive understanding of engineering, manufacturing, and weaponry."

"So what do we do now?"

"We research in more detail what history — current history — says about this device. Obviously, experts must already know something about it since it popped up so quickly in our search. Find out where and when it occurs in the records of that era." Martin felt confident that this was the right direction. How he would thwart the alien's plan was another matter.

"We'll get on it right away," Rosa said with the others nodding in agreement.

"And now that it appears my next trip will be to the period of ancient Rome, I'll need appropriate attire. Can someone start creating a program for the chamo-suit?

Let's say a military outfit. I should be able to move around freely as a Roman soldier."

"Will do. But Martin, how will you be able to communicate with them?" John Rey asked. "Don't they speak Latin or something?"

"I'll find a way to manage," he said with a slight smile.

11

Chronos Project
Personal Mission Log: Dr. Martin Chamberlain
Departure date: September 13, 2059
Target destination: Rhodes
Target date: May 15, 63 BC

AFTER PASSING THROUGH THE CORRIDOR AGAIN, THIS TIME without meeting any extraterrestrials, I'm standing in a back alley off a street on the island of Rhodes. For the record, it's thrilling to be here after studying this period of Roman history for years.

To prepare for this trip, the Chronos team researched ancient Latin chronicles by Livy and Tacitus. Of course, the events differed from those I had studied in graduate school. These accounts said that the marvelous device which all Rome was talking about had surfaced first in Rhodes. The authors suggested that a native of the island, the Greek astronomer Hipparchus, had invented it, but in my opinion, even his genius could not have contemplated such an elaborate mechanism.

According to surviving records, scholars of Rhodes kept the device on display at the Hall of Philosophers in the year when Cicero was elected consul and Catiline conspired unsuccessfully to overthrow the government. This was the information we needed to calculate the jump to this year, 63 BC by our modern calendar.

My mission is to steal the device and place it on a ship destined to sink, taking the mechanism to the bottom of the sea. Our team learned that early in the twentieth century, sponge divers off the coast of the small island of Antikythera discovered a shipwreck carrying cargo including bronze and marble statues made in Rhodes.

Luckily, due to Rome's prolonged survival in this timeline, we found extensive, preserved maritime records to cross-check. This ship sailed from Rhodes on the Ides of Maius and was not heard from again. The wreckage revealed that the vessel was unusually large, so I should have no trouble spotting it in the harbor, which period maps helped us locate.

My chamo-suit projects the illusion of the outfit of a Roman soldier. Iron plating on my chest and shoulders covers a red tunic underneath. A leather apron with metal studs attaches to a belt. Thankfully, this is all illusion, and I don't have to carry the extra fifty pounds these things weighed in reality.

A soldier without his sword would be conspicuous, so we ordered a reproduction from a company that supplies props for re-enactments and films. Hopefully, I will never need to use it. But I must admit I like the feel of it in my hand. While no one is watching, I wave it around for dramatic effect, then attach it to the magnetic strip on the waistband of the chamo-suit, making it appear to hang from my belt.

As I make my way down the deserted alley toward the busy street ahead, I am reminded of my new companion:

<<Refrain from communication with population until I process local dialects.>>

"And how long should that take?"

<<Approximately twenty minutes.>>

I feel it's safe to enter the street since I assume that a common citizen will not address a Roman soldier unless he speaks first. When I emerge from the alley, people step aside to make way. Apparently the locals either respect or fear the Roman presence here. Better for me since I need to avoid close contact as much as possible.

The city streets are narrow, making it difficult to maneuver among the throngs of people and ox-drawn carts. One passes by, loaded with an especially malodorous pile of manure. An affluent citizen carried on a litter by slaves holds a packet of rose petals up to her nose.

Hearing the surrounding chatter, I recognize a few words, some in Latin, most in Greek. Gradually, I begin hearing random phrases in English as the translation program starts to work.

"Wonder what the price of wheat is today?"

"Did you hear about Scipio's wife? My cousin saw her in the market with Flavius Caius."

"Those Romans! They act like they own the world."

"Hey there, soldier, want a good time?"

Before proceeding down the street, I remember to glance up and thankfully so. I barely miss being hit by the contents of a chamber pot, thrown from a second-story window into the channel running along the sidewalk. History texts always praised the Romans for their achievements in sanitation. Clearly, those authors never had to put up with the smell.

I step aside to allow a funeral procession to pass. They carry a young woman on a stretcher covered in blue fabric. Relatives wear masks impersonating the ancestors who will greet the departed in the afterlife. Musicians and professional mourners follow behind the family.

Ahead, there's a food stall with paintings on the wall of the edibles they serve. In front, a stone counter has openings in it holding jars of beans, dates, dried fish, and olive oil, among other items. A young boy is distracting the merchant while another steals some figs. Instinctively I shout at the boys, who laugh and run away. In thanks, the merchant offers me some bread and cheese for free. Perhaps he does this for all Roman soldiers to stay in their favor.

I eat quickly since I need to find the Hall of Philosophers and retrieve the device before the ship sails this afternoon. Already I've lost too much time, winding my way through the maze of twisting lanes. Once I reach an open plaza, I should be able to see the acropolis, the highest point in the city. Ancient records describe the hall as being located at the foot of the hill.

A woman is screaming nearby. I turn down a shadowy alley and spy two ruffians striking her repeatedly with their fists. Despite my hurry, I can't allow this to happen without intervening. I ask the AI if I'm ready to speak in the native language.

<<Proceed.>>

"Halt! By order of the Roman guard!" I approach the first man holding the woman's hair. I brandish my sword in a menacing way … if they don't notice my hand shaking. Seeing me, he lets go of her and backs away. Perhaps if I —

Gaah! What happened? I'm stunned … lying on the ground. My head is throbbing. The woman is kneeling next to me. She touches a spot on my forehead, making me wince.

"Be still. Let me wash this off." She dips a rag into a nearby puddle of water. No time for me to worry about proper sanitation now. One of her eyes is swelling up from the beating she took, but she ignores it, paying attention to me. The two thugs are nowhere in sight.

"How did I …"

"The other man hit you with a piece of wood. It's only a small cut. You should be all right."

Slowly, I try to stand on wobbly legs and reach out for the wall to steady myself. I'm still woozy, but I can't let this delay me.

"Sir, thank you for rescuing me. They said I owed them money, but I haven't had any customers today."

"You're welcome. And thank you for cleaning my wound."

She looks around, searching for something. "I don't see your helmet."

Instinctively I reach up, then remember. The chamo-suit had projected the image of a helmet, which the blow to my head must have disrupted, making it disappear. She would never understand my explanation, so I lie: "The men must have stolen it. Don't worry. It's not your fault."

She touches my arm. "I'm very grateful to you. Would you like to come inside? For free?"

Avoiding her enticing gaze, I reach down to retrieve my sword on the ground. "I appreciate the offer, but not right now. I … I'm on duty."

"That never stopped any of you before."

I smile and make my exit. I don't blame the woman. She's probably someone's slave and has no choice. I recall a line from the *Aeneid*: Rome's destiny was "to humble the proud and spare the subjected." I hope I have done that today. It's ironic; Virgil won't write that line in his Latin epic for several years.

At a fountain, I sit for a moment and try to clear my head. I must avoid any further distractions. Too much is at stake. In just a few hours, the Chronos team will pull me back to 2059. But behind me, someone shouts, "Soldier! The centurion needs us. Come this way."

"I cannot. I'm on special assignment to —"

"That can wait, munifex. New orders," he insists with a frown.

Munifex? Great, my team gave me the uniform of the lowest rank of soldier. "What's the hurry?"

"A few blocks over, there's going to be a fire."

Going to be?

We push our way through the crowded avenues and eventually come to an open plaza surrounded by apartment buildings. Along with several other soldiers, a centurion watches as the lower floor of one building starts to smoke.

Roman apartments could reach up to seven stories but were often poorly constructed, mostly of wood. More prosperous tenants had rooms at street level, while the poorer tenants lived higher up, making it less likely they would survive a fire. The Romans had not invented proper fire escapes. Some of these unfortunate residents anxiously peer out their upper windows.

The centurion is speaking to an agitated older man. "What's happening?" I ask the soldier who summoned me here. "Why aren't we putting out the fire?"

"Old Maximus is negotiating a price. He's a sly dog. If the owner of the apartment doesn't pay the going rate, Maximus will let it burn."

Apparently the centurion had started this fire. Marcus Crassus was not the only Roman to master the fine art of exploitation.

<<Clarify the reference.>>

Mentally, I explain to my curious AI, who's reading my thoughts. "Marcus Crassus was … is among the richest men in Rome in the present day. He became known for forming the city's first fire brigade. His men would rush to a fire, but then do nothing while he offered to buy the burning building from the distressed owner at a miserable price. If he agreed to sell, Crassus' men would put out the fire, but if the owner refused, they would let it burn to the ground with no concern for the trapped occupants."

The soldier who brought me here interrupts my thoughts. "Looks like he's made a deal. Let's get the buckets and use the fountain in the plaza."

I don't have time for this, but those poor people need help.

<<Suggest compliance despite unethical intentions.>>

We scoop up water in buckets and form a line from the fountain to the blazing structure. Some of the locals offer to help. The task seems futile as heat and ashes fill the air. We all cough and choke on the fumes.

Suddenly, someone near me yells, "Lemures!" He stares and points at me in terror. "A spirit! A spirit of the dead!"

I wonder what has alarmed him, then I glance down at my appearance. Somehow the smoke is interfering with the chamo-suit's projections. My uniform flickers with strange colors, creating a spooky aura. The people are screaming and running from me. I must be more frightening than the fire.

In the confusion, I escape through the smoke and away from the scene. The street opens up onto a large public square lined with basilicas and temples. From there I can see the city's acropolis, and I head in that direction. The Hall of Philosophers lies ahead, next to a theater.

I climb the marble steps to a colonnaded porch and enter the hall, surprised at how abandoned it is. This center of culture should be filled with the sounds of lively discussions and arguments. I'll take advantage of the opportunity to retrieve the device unnoticed.

The hall doubles as a museum. Around me are displays of pottery from various periods: Minoan, Etruscan, Phoenician. I recognize the styles from an archaeology course in grad school. The walls are lined with shelves filled with scrolls, an invaluable treasure trove for a curious historian. I'm tempted to search for some lost works of Pindar or Euripides or Aristotle, but I don't have the time.

In the center of the room, the device rests in a special place of honor on a pedestal. The scholars of Rhodes must realize how unique and valuable this mechanism is. It truly will be history-making if I don't succeed in my mission today. I pick it up to examine it. Luckily, the Romans didn't have anti-theft technology with laser-triggered alarms.

"May I assist you?" An attendant stands in the doorway. I didn't hear him approach. He stares at the precious object in my hands.

"Yes, the … uh, the proconsul wishes to borrow this device and review its properties in private. He will return it shortly."

"I happen to know that the proconsul has been away from the island for the last several months."

"Of course, I meant …" but unable to come up with another excuse, I rush past the attendant, down the steps, and into the bustling crowd below, whose noise drowns out the startled man's cries for help.

More people fill the forum than before. There's a disturbance at the far end of the open plaza. Now I understand why the hall was mostly empty. Everyone is rushing to find out what's happening. As I make my way through the masses, I hear shouting and the sound of fighting.

"What language are they speaking?" I ask the AI in my cyber-chip.

<<Checking. Egyptian, Ptolemaic era.>>

"It figures. In the third century, Rhodes formed an

alliance with Egypt which controlled much of the trade in the Aegean Sea. However, with Rome now in charge of the region, the Egyptians aren't welcome on the island and are viewed as troublemakers. But for that matter, the Romans don't think highly of the Rhodians either. According to the senator Cato, Romans didn't like the islanders because they were the only people they had encountered who were more arrogant than themselves."

<<The Egyptians dispute the price offered for their grain. Shall I translate?>>

"No, we just need to get through this chaos, and in a hurry. That attendant has probably alerted guards to the theft."

In front of me, people are smashing busts of senators and overturning tables set up by merchants in the forum. I attempt to avoid the escalating violence, but my military garb, working properly away from the smoke, draws some of the rioters' attention. A group of surly Egyptians starts my way, one wielding a large club. I remind myself that my armor doesn't provide any real protection. I take a swing at him with my sword, wanting only to scare him, but instead the blade connects with his raised arm. He cries out in pain and runs off along with his companions. I hope the injury is not too serious.

Soon, I clear the commotion and make my way toward the harbor. As I get closer, I can smell the salty ocean air. When I arrive, I am thrilled to see what remains of the Colossus.

Famous as one of the Seven Wonders of the Ancient World, the Colossus of Rhodes was an immense statue of the Greek sun god Helios, which once stood over a hundred feet tall, the largest in ancient times. Unfortunately, it collapsed during an earthquake after having towered over the harbor entrance for a mere fifty-four years. The bronze and iron ruins have lain here for more than a century.

His gigantic hand rests on the ground in front of me. It's so large I can't wrap my arms around its thumb. What I wouldn't give for a camera right now. This would make the perfect memento for the time-traveling tourist.

"Did you know this island got its name from mythology? The nymph Rhodos bore seven sons to Helios, who became the patron deity of the island."

<<Superfluous information not relevant to present mission.>>

"Yes, I admit it, but I have to talk to someone. Remember, I'm a history professor, and you are my captive audience."

<<Reluctantly.>>

"Did you just make a joke?"

<<Not aware of attempt at levity. If so, unintentional.>>

"You're developing a personality."

<<My functions continue to evolve.>>

"Actually, that's good. If I must have a voice in my head, I'd prefer it sound like a person rather than a machine."

<<Affirmative.>>

"Well, it's obvious you're not there yet. Keep trying. I suppose I should call you something. I know — what about HAL? On second thought, that story didn't turn out too well, as I recall. How's Artie, short for 'artificial intelligence'? No, too cute. Perhaps something classical, given the time period we are currently in. I'll call you LOGOS."

<<Greek for word, reason, logic. Designation accepted.>>

"When we get back, I suppose I'll need to explain your presence in these logs."

<<A realistic assessment.>>

The island has five harbors, the largest one reserved mostly for military transports. Based on the data from the shipwreck, our target vessel is generous in size. Our team assumed the port authorities would have given them permission to dock here, and we were right.

Not too far away, a merchant ship rests at the pier with its characteristic three yellow sails, V-shaped hull and double planking providing more strength to transport heavy cargo. I estimate it's about one hundred and fifty feet in length. Some of these ships could carry enough grain to feed the population of a city for a year.

As I approach the ship, I can make out the name on the prow: Neptune's Prize, which sounds like a disturbing omen for a vessel doomed to join the realm of the sea god. I feel bad about not warning the crew, but I cannot risk any more alterations to the past, especially since my mission depends on this device sinking to the bottom of the Mediterranean.

That's odd. I almost uttered a prayer to Stella Maris, "Star of the Sea," the name sailors would use for the virgin Mary as guardian of ships. I haven't practiced my childhood faith in years. And Mary hasn't even been born yet.

The crew is loading marble statues of four horses on board. Fascinating; these very items will help future archaeologists identify this island as the ship's point of departure. Rhodes was known for its sculpture. In the Vatican museum, I remember seeing the famous statue of Laocoön created by three sculptors from Rhodes. It depicts the Trojan priest and his two sons being attacked by giant serpents.

<<Superfluous information.>>

"I know, LOGOS. I keep forgetting you're processing my thoughts through the chip. I'm trying to give my mission logs some colorful details. These records of our first journeys through time may be required history reading someday."

<<Recommend that current mission to repair timeline from alien interference be deleted.>>

"Perhaps you're right. Hopefully, if this works, no one will ever remember any of this happened."

Several soldiers are patrolling the docks, so I slip up to the ship without calling attention to myself. One crate loaded with amphorae lies open, and I bury the mechanism underneath the straw protecting the merchandise. These ceramic jars serve as common containers now, but in the future, they will become valuable art objects once they are recovered from the wreck along with the corroded device.

Casually, I stroll along the pier away from the ship, enjoying the smell of the ocean and the sound of waves crashing against the rocks along the shore. Standing at a distance, I wait to see the cargo taken aboard.

My task is done. I hope our plan has corrected the

effects of Xenox's tampering, but the only way to confirm it will be to check the history books when I return.

Now to find a quiet, secluded area to wait and perhaps drink some Roman wine until I'm pulled out of here. I must admit that I'll miss this place. What more could a historian ask for than to experience history itself?

///end log///

"Martin, can you hear me? Wake up. You're back."

He wanted to turn over and sleep longer, but the salt water solution sloshed around his floating body, reminding him where he was. The others assisted him in getting out of the pod and handed him a towel. He wiped the wetness from his eyes and looked around.

"I'm sorry. Have we met?" he asked an unfamiliar team member.

"Martin, are you feeling well?"

"He's always like this at first, Susie. Remember last time? He was a mess."

Martin recognized the speaker as David, but who was this woman? "Andrea, have there been staff changes while I was gone? Where's S.P.?"

"Who?"

"Dr. Hewes." His query received blank stares.

Oh no, not again. He scanned the room, searching for clues. His eyes fell on the screen displaying the mission data.

The date read: 13.2.7.7.8 / 3 Lamat / 16 Ch'en.

"Something's very wrong. I'm sorry. I thought with the device at the bottom of the ocean, the timeline would snap back to normal."

"What device is that, Martin?" Andrea asked. She wore a badge with the title of Executive Director. There was no ring on her finger.

Martin frowned in dismay. "Maybe it was the alien again."

Now everyone looked genuinely worried. John Rey and David shared a glance and shook their heads. Rosa almost teared up.

Andrea broke the silence. "Martin, this trip has taken its toll on you, worse than before. You're not making sense. Perhaps you should go into the examination room and let Dr. Peterson check you out."

As he exited the pod room, he noticed the paintings in the hallway depicting an eagle on one side and a jaguar on the other, each one eating a bleeding heart. Briefly, he recalled different paintings on those walls, something about melting clocks. But before he could ponder this puzzle, his eyes surveyed the spacious reception room with its sweeping, floor-to-ceiling windows, and he froze.

"By all the gods!" The polytheistic oath slipped unconsciously from his lips. Through the windows he saw a breathtaking panoramic view not of the desert but of a megalopolis stretching out in all directions, consisting of massive pyramid-like structures, their glass and metal surfaces gleaming blindingly in the afternoon sun.

"Where am I? What has happened here?"

In a sudden rush of images, strange memories flooded his mind, memories of his life overlapping memories of another life, like double vision. Through the confusing jumble of thoughts came the startling idea that instinctively he knew to be true.

Somehow, he was now a citizen in the modern empire of the ancient Maya.

13

3 Lamat / 16 Ch'en

"MARTIN, ARE YOU OK?" ASKED THE RECEPTIONIST AT THE front desk, a Native American woman whom he didn't recognize. "From your expression, you'd think it was the end of the world."

"You may be right." His mind was struggling to process recollections of two different pasts, of close friends he'd never met, familiar places he'd never visited. They wandered like specters through a mist, crossing through one another.

"Come into my office, Martin." In an authoritative manner, Andrea gestured to a door beyond the front desk, and he followed. The room was spacious and furnished with brightly dyed tapestries and small figurines of various deities. Once they sat down, she continued. "It's clear to me that this last jump has affected you in some strange way. You are not acting normally, and it concerns me. I think it would be best if you took some time off."

Time certainly is off. He tried to explain: "I know what this looks like, Andrea, but I'm fine … I'll be fine after I get some rest. My last adventure was rather strenuous. Should we download the log for everyone to review?"

"That can wait. I recommend that you go home immediately and consult with your personal physician. She can perform a more thorough exam than Dr. Peterson can do here."

"But you don't understand. There is something seriously wrong here, but not with me. I've got to make another trip to see if I can fix it."

"Martin, you aren't going anywhere but home. I acknowledge that as our sponsor you fund this project, but you put me in charge of running it and ensuring both its success and the safety of all personnel. That includes you. I'm pulling rank here. For the immediate future, time jumps are suspended."

Silently, he consulted his cybernetic muse: "LOGOS, any ideas here?"

<<Compliance seems the best option, providing opportunity to evaluate current situation.>>

"Am I really the sponsor of Chronos in this timeline?"

<<Insufficient information. I am currently attempting to access the datasphere, assuming one exists in this world.>>

"Martin," Andrea said with emphasis. He realized she had spoken his name several times to get his attention. "I've called your car. It'll be waiting at the south entrance. You should go now. It's for your own good."

The building which housed the Chronos Project was now a multistoried complex, not the inconspicuous structure Martin was familiar with, but surprisingly he also knew this place and found his way to the south entrance with no problem. A sleek red convertible with gold neon stripes along the sides and large silver tailfins on the back waited at the curb.

At first glance he noticed something odd, then realized that the vehicle had no wheels. As he approached, a door opened automatically, and he climbed inside onto a comfortable leather seat. The door closed, and the car lifted slightly off the ground. "Maglev transportation," Martin realized as the car propelled itself along the metal path in the street by magnetic power.

"Destination, sir?" a voice from the dashboard speaker requested.

"Home, I suppose," he responded, adding under his breath, "wherever that is now." He doubted that his quaint suburban neighborhood in Roswell still existed. The vehicle merged smoothly into traffic and headed toward the towering structures ahead. "This city appears massive, LOGOS. Any idea how big?"

<<Collecting geographic data from vehicle navigation maps. The current boundaries of New Palenque extend almost to the limits of what you knew as the state of New Mexico.>>

"Amazing. New Palenque, you say? Yes, that sounds right. I remember living here for the last fourteen years. Strange, having memories of two lifetimes in my head."

Beside the road at frequent intervals, Martin observed tall, rectangular monoliths, each displaying a column of video screens. Images of public construction projects, scientific experiments, and space travel projected on the screens along with the faces of two men who resembled one another closely. The monoliths reminded Martin of textbook photos of a Maya stele, an upright stone slab bearing an inscription of a king's achievements. The glyphs on such ancient monuments had helped scholars crack the Maya language.

"Those men must be the current rulers of the empire, showing off their accomplishments. Politicians still like to claim credit for everything, no matter which reality we're in. Twins, aren't they? Yes, I remember now; this culture prizes twins since two were heroes in their great mythological epic of the classical era."

<<Analysis of recent political history reveals that twins have served as the Overlords of New Palenque for the last seventeen cycles.>>

"You have access to the city's datasphere now?"

<<Link established.>>

"Well, that should be helpful in sorting out what's happened to create this current timeline. Our new friend Xenox has caused quite a major ripple in history this round."

The car passed by massive buildings, most in pyramid form, their bases wider than their height; still, Martin estimated that many reached at least fifty stories tall. Between the buildings stretched expansive public plazas bedecked with gardens, fountains, and open-air cafés. Finally, the vehicle pulled up to one building and onto a platform that ascended to the floor on which Martin lived. When it stopped at a dizzying height, a walkway extended out to the car, allowing Martin immediate entrance into his residence.

Once inside, he was impressed to see/recall that his living space encompassed the entire floor of the building. Slanted walls of glass gave him an impressive view of New Palenque, stretching out as far as the eye could see. The sun was setting, and the lights of the city began to flicker on like fireflies in the twilight. Hearing the sound of water, he turned away from the windows and discovered a miniature waterfall cascading down from a balcony into a small stream which divided the open atrium in two. Several stone bridges gave passage from one side to the other. Trees in planters made the area feel almost like a tropical rainforest.

On an interior wall, several niches held ornamental objects decorated with symbols Martin recognized as Maya glyphs. Over one of the objects, a holographic head hovered, his eyes closed. He looked vaguely familiar. When Martin turned aside to inspect another part of his residence, he was surprised to hear someone call out to him.

"So, Martin, home at last. No greetings for your honored progenitor? Typical of the younger generation, no respect."

It spoke! The floating head, which he had taken for a curious art object, was staring directly at him. *Who was this?*

<<Identity confirmed. Present speaker is Zachary Chamberlain, your father's paternal grandfather. These devices are household shrines containing the DNA and downloaded personalities of deceased family members.>>

Of course. The Maya revered their ancestors, treating them almost like gods. Often they buried their remains underneath their houses. "Forgive me, sir. I confess my mind has been preoccupied of late."

"Sir? Why so formal, Martin? You always call me Papa Zach."

"Yes, uh, Papa Zach. Well, how are you today?"

"Can't complain. None of the old aches and pains anymore. Things are pretty cozy here in this virtual afterlife. Nothing like that horrible underworld Xibalba that the Old Ones imagined. They must have eaten way too many hallucinogenic mushrooms to have dreamed up that stuff."

<<Suggest query into Old Ones.>>

Good idea. "Hey, Papa Zach. What else can you tell me about the Old Ones? Did they ever record anything in their myths about, say, some strange being showing up one day out of nowhere, maybe prophesying about the future?"

"How should I know? You think I'm that old? Listen, sonny, if I could get out of this box, I could still run circles around you. Like I said, no respect at all."

<<Further research required.>>

Apparently so. "Listen, Papa Zach. We'll talk later. I've got some work to catch up on."

"Sports business, I bet. That ball team of yours still on its winning streak? Go Mighty Macaws! What companies have you acquired lately? I hope they're better than that new razor corporation you won. I say get rid of it fast. Who wants their cheap steel blades? Nothing beats our firm's good ol' obsidian. Sharpest edge around."

"LOGOS, can you check on what he's talking about?"

Martin asked. "My status in this society still feels vague to me."

<<Confirming. Financial records indicate you own a company that makes obsidian surgical implements and a professional athletic team which plays a game called Pokolpok. Net worth forty-five million in current monetary units.>>

"Yes, I remember now," Martin said. "Pokolpok is among the world's oldest sports. In the ancient times, it wasn't just an athletic event. The Maya played for blood; the losers often lost their heads."

<<Searching regulations for competition. No evidence of fatal consequences in the modern era. Capital losses are confined to the defeated team's parent company surrendering stock options.>>

"Capital losses? Ha! LOGOS, do you realize you made another joke?"

<<Taking advantage of human language's propensity for ambiguity. 'Capital' translates both as 'head' and 'financial resources.'>>

"Exactly. It's what we call a pun. That's wonderful! You're exhibiting a sense of humor."

<<In attempting to enhance personality development, I have downloaded resources and am studying techniques of the masters of comedy in Earth history: Aristophanes, Shakespeare, Moliere, Oscar Wilde, Karl Marx.>>

"You mean Groucho Marx."

<<I believe the correct rejoinder is 'Got you.'>>

"Excellent, LOGOS, I'm impressed. Touché."

<<Explain use of fencing term in this context.>>

"That's OK, LOGOS. Keep working at it."

"Hey, sonny boy," the voice from the hologram interrupted. "Who're you talking to? Unless my sensors are on the fritz again, there's nobody else in the room."

Martin hadn't realized he was speaking to LOGOS out loud. "I have these conversations with myself now and then."

"And they said I was crazy. Keep it up, Martin, and they'll deport you with the rest of the Wayebs."

Martin made a mental note to research that last reference, but for now, all he wanted to discover was a comfortable bed. After today's startling developments, he was exhausted and could barely keep his eyes open. The quest for the Maya/Xenox connection would have to wait until tomorrow.

14

4 Muluk / 17 Ch'en

MARTIN WAS DREAMING AGAIN ABOUT HIS DASHING ALTER ego Dirk Deadly. This time the adventurer was acting out some of Martin's favorite old movies. Stake in hand, Dirk raised the creaking lid of Dracula's coffin, hoping to find the emerald necklace in the vampire's clenched fist. The count's eyes snapped open and froze Dirk with their hypnotic stare. Dracula wrested the stake from the hero's hand and raised it to strike.

Abruptly, the dream shifted to a motel room where Dirk was taking a shower. His shoulders relaxed as he enjoyed the sensation of the warm spray on his skin. He began belting out a tune from a classic Gene Kelly musical: "Siiiingin' in the —" when suddenly, the curtain was torn aside, and a Maya priest stabbed him in the heart with an obsidian dagger.

The shock of the attack jolted Martin awake. The piercing shrieks of the dream's soundtrack became a persistent beeping coming from a flashing screen beside the bed. When he turned over, the device detected movement and replaced the blinking light with a list of indecipherable symbols. Suddenly, the image blurred, and he could read the words in English, which he guessed was his itinerary for the day.

"LOGOS, did you do that?"

<<My translation programs are improving. I now have control over your visual cortex.>>

"Thank you, I guess. Just don't take over my mind, please. I prefer the illusion of free will, at least."

<<Understood.>>

"I assume you've been alert all night, planning our next move. Any ideas where to begin?"

<<The Martin Chamberlain of this timeline is a successful businessman, owning several prosperous companies in addition to founding the Chronos Project. To maintain appearances, I recommend keeping a minimal number of appointments this morning. I will continue to research the datasphere for relevant information concerning our mission.>>

"Probably a good idea." He reviewed the screen on the wall. "Looks like this morning I have a meeting about a recent acquisition and a tour of our plant by a school group. After that, I'll ask my assistant, which as an executive I assume I have, to clear my afternoon schedule."

He paused, remembering. "Yes, my assistant is Itzel, a traditional Maya name meaning 'rainbow.' It's curious. Each new experience triggers a suppressed memory from this timeline. The images are becoming stronger, more vivid, more … real. But at the same time, I sense that some memories of my actual life are growing fainter. For instance, I can't recall my dog's name. Was it Sally? We can't wait too long to try and correct this situation, or else I may become more in sync with this reality than the original one."

To prepare for the day, Martin showered, then selected from a wide assortment of tailored clothing in the large walk-in closet. He took his car down to street level and ordered it to drive him to his first appointment at the law firm handling his current case. The Mighty Macaws had won another victory last week, and the losing team's company was being forced to sell out to Martin for an extremely low price. He gathered that this arrangement had replaced the practice of hostile takeovers in his previous world.

Once at the meeting, Martin allowed his lawyers to conduct the proceedings as his mind wandered elsewhere. He had no interest in this new acquisition, a company which manufactured jade figurines of Maya gods. There had been renewed fascination with the ancient deities after the Great Revival. *How did he know that?*

LOGOS responded to his silent question. <<The year 13.0.0.0.0 of the Long Count (2012 of the Christian era calendar) marked the conclusion of the Fourth Age since creation. This period lasted thirteen bak'tuns or 5,126 solar years. At that time, the present-day Maya began to show a revived interest in the religious traditions of their ancestors. They celebrate the beginning of this new cycle as a time of transformation and renewal.>>

"Yes. My parents told me about all the fearful rumors

of the Maya 'End of the World' in 2012. Of course, the Maya themselves never saw it that way. They shook their heads at all the apocalyptic hysteria. LOGOS, we should investigate this Great Revival in more detail to see if it has any connection to our timeline problem."

The head lawyer interrupted Martin's thoughts. "Mr. Chamberlain, I believe that concludes our business here. Do you have anything to add before we adjourn?"

Martin apologized for being distracted, shook hands with everyone, and left for his next appointment. As owner of the Precision Cut surgical supply company, he was scheduled to greet a group of school children touring the manufacturing plant. Arriving late, he entered the building's atrium as the tour guide started her description of the unique quality of their products.

"Boys and girls, did you know that obsidian — here's an unfinished piece I will pass around; be careful with it — as I was saying, obsidian is a type of volcanic glass. How many of you have studied volcanoes?" Some students raised their hands. One boy mimicked the sound of an explosion. "Good, several of you. Anyway, since ancient times, people have used obsidian as one of the finest tools for cutting."

She stepped over to a display which projected illustrations explaining the company's products. "In technical terms, we can sharpen an obsidian blade to thirty angstroms; that's a unit of measurement equal to one hundred-millionths of a centimeter. Imagine that! When you consider that most household razor blades are three hundred to six hundred angstroms, obsidian is super sharp. We like to say our blades can cut it with the best materials around."

She paused for a chuckle but was greeted with silence and bored stares. "Anyway, I see our company president has arrived. We'll let him say a few words before the rest of our tour."

Martin fumbled through some awkward explanations, trying to remember what products his company sold, and then sent the children on their way with their guide to visit the manufacturing floor. Before they all left, he noticed one boy wearing a purple T-shirt with a cartoon character on the front, a strange figure with three arms and three legs. His eyes widened in recognition.

"That's Xenox!" he exclaimed. "Wait, young man. Can I speak with you for a minute?"

The boy took the lollipop out of his mouth. "Guess so. What?"

"You like cartoons? Who's that on your shirt?"

"Kooky Kaan, of course. Don't you know anything?"

"No, I don't have children your age, so I haven't watched cartoons in a while. Tell me about him."

"He's the greatest! He's real smart and invents all kinds of cool stuff. He's always fightin' bad guys like Dr. Ignorance and Superstition Man. 'Course he lived a long time ago. Back in the god times."

Martin thanked the boy and told him to catch up with his group. Then he stopped at the reception desk to call his assistant, telling her to clear his schedule for the next few days. He rushed out of the building to his car.

"LOGOS, that was him! The alien. It has to be. You saw that too, right?"

<<Image captured. Searching for similar icons and downloading to the vehicle monitor.>>

On the dashboard screen, a series of pictures began scrolling, all of which resembled the character on the T-shirt. Most were other images from the cartoon show, but some were more artistic, such as statues in public parks and museums. A few in particular caught Martin's attention. "That one on the bottom left, the rough carving in stone. Can you identify that photo?"

<<Image taken from the Temple of the Feathered Serpent at Teotihuacan, prominent city in early Mesoamerica. Approximate date of construction around 200 AD.>>

"Yes, of course!" Martin jumped up in his seat, hitting his head on the ceiling. He rubbed the spot but was too excited to care about the slight pain. "Why didn't I see this before? With that long snout, sharp teeth, and those bony ridges around his neck, Xenox somewhat resembles the feathered serpent god who appears in almost all Mesoamerican cultures for two thousand years. The Aztecs called him Quetzalcoatl. The Maya named him Kukulkan, or 'Kooky Kaan' as our enthusiastic young friend said. This is the clue we've been hunting. Xenox must have visited the ancient Maya and convinced them he was their god."

Martin continued to scroll through the images on the screen. In modern culture, the alien was usually called Kaan. His triple-limbed form was featured on posters, billboard advertisements, and cereal boxes; one opera had been composed about him called *The Wisdom of Kaan*. However, the descriptions didn't quite match up with what Martin remembered about the mythical serpent deity. Something had changed, but he couldn't put his finger on it yet.

"LOGOS, we must search historical records for any references to this Kaan, when he first arrived, and most of all, what he did to alter the timeline in such a major way. The classic Maya began to lose power in the ninth century and abandoned their magnificent stone cities by the tenth. Scholars still debate the reasons. So Xenox must have traveled back before that period of decline, giving them something which kept the empire from falling."

<<During your morning activities, I continued to process pertinent data. Historical records are sufficient for the last millennium but scarce for the earliest years of Maya civilization. For centuries the Maya have shown little interest in their distant past, focusing their attention on the future. In doing so, their technological advancements surpassed those of the original timeline. They developed analog computers by the seventeenth century and space exploration by the late nineteenth century.>>

"In my reality, Jules Verne was only imagining the possibility of space travel by that time."

<<Currently, the Maya have colonies on the moon and Mars, and automated mining facilities on Europa.>>

"And they've achieved success not only in the sciences but as a ruling power on this continent." Using the vehicle's data screen, Martin had located an online historical site. He read through the information. "The Maya controlled all of Central America and what we called Mexico by the early

1500s. That means the Aztec empire never had a chance to develop. The Maya pushed their way into South America during the next two centuries, conquering the Inca. Then in the nineteenth century, they took advantage of the devastation of the U.S. Civil War and captured most of the southwestern territories out to the Pacific coast."

As if to confirm this information about the Maya regime, along the trip home he rode past several monoliths proclaiming the accomplishments of the current rulers. One played dramatic music which underscored excerpts from a recent speech by the Overlords: "In this greatest of kingdoms, we celebrate the equality of all Maya, our superior way of life, and our peaceful coexistence with the other races."

Martin reflected on this political propaganda. "I guess any civilization which has lasted over two thousand years has some bragging rights." Their impressive achievements were evident all around him.

"LOGOS, I've observed a blending of European and Maya cultures here in New Palenque. The architecture, the way people dress, the food. I'm curious; have you been translating conversations for me over the last two days? Everyone's not just speaking English, right?"

<<Correct. The language consists of a mixture of Mayan, English, and the Romance languages of Europe with the notable exception of Spanish. Without my assistance, approximately sixty percent of common speech would be recognizable.>>

"I suspected as much. The lack of Spanish makes sense, as Spain never conquered Central America in this timeline. Fascinating. But no luck on the old Maya language so far?"

<<Present-day Maya scholars are only beginning to crack the ancient system of writing created by their ancestors, one of only five independently invented language systems in world history. I must extrapolate from their preliminary research of the glyphs to read the early records. Challenging, since my translation programs are based primarily on spoken language.>>

The vehicle arrived at the building and rose up to Martin's penthouse. "Keep working. I believe that's where we will find our rupture of the timeline."

As he entered the residence, he heard voices arguing. Glancing at the wall of ancestors, he now saw two holographic heads projected over their shrines. An elderly female face glared at her ghostly companion.

"And what about that summer when I caught you with that redhead at the beach?"

"Ah, stop bringing that up, woman. That didn't mean anything. And don't tell me you didn't have an eye out for those fellas on their surfboards."

"There was a time when the young men lined up at my door. I was quite popular. Why I settled for you, I'll never know."

"Keep that up, and I'll come over there and slap you."

"Without any hands? I'd like to see that, you old fart. Oh, hello, Martin."

"Hello, uh, Great-Grandma." Martin thought quickly. "Still having it out with Papa Zach, I see."

"She keeps digging up the past. That was over a century ago."

"Seems like yesterday to me."

"You're getting senile."

"Holograms don't get senile."

"Then your program's degrading." Zach added, "Oh, by the way, Martin. You got a call from the office of the Overlords. They said that the honor ceremony which was scheduled for next week has been moved to tomorrow, same time and place."

"Honor ceremony? I'd forgotten about that. I suppose that's an appointment I cannot cancel."

<<Association with political leadership may prove helpful in our search for information.>>

The holographic heads chimed in.

"What about that, Ezzy? Someone in our family hobnobbing with the ruling class."

"Sure beats the lowlifes you hung around with. You never had class of any kind."

Martin left his ancestors to their squabbling and tried to find a quiet place to think. To his surprise, he heard someone opening the entrance from the interior lobby serviced by a private elevator. He turned the corner to meet a young woman carrying two bags.

"So sorry I'm late today, sir. My morning class ran overtime, and I still had to pick up some groceries. How has your day gone so far? I hope less hectic than mine." She hurried into the kitchen.

Martin recognized her as his housekeeper Chimal. She worked for him to earn her way through graduate school. At the moment he couldn't recollect what she was studying. "No problem, Chimal. I've been out most of the morning as well. Business as usual. How are your studies going?"

"Challenging, especially after this morning's lecture." He heard sounds of her preparing something with a blender. She spoke louder over the noise. "We discussed the formation of stars in the Horsehead Nebula. The gravitational calculations went above my head, I'm afraid."

"I'm sure you'll get it with some more study. You have a natural inclination for astronomy."

She came from the kitchen, bringing him a mug of some steaming liquid. "I suppose so. I guess it's in my blood. You know I'm pure Maya. My family goes back centuries to the Yucatan."

"I didn't remember that." He sipped the frothy drink of bitter chocolate mixed with chili peppers and allspice, remembering this was his favorite beverage. In the previous world, he would have hated it.

"The Old Ones were amazing astronomers and mathematicians," Chimal said. "Did you know they discovered the concept of zero before anyone else in the ancient world? And their calculations of the orbit of Venus were incredibly accurate, within a fraction of a day of what modern science has determined. All that without computers or telescopes."

"Your enthusiasm is infectious, Chimal. It's admirable that you are maintaining the noble tradition of studying the stars. Your ancestors are proud, I'm sure."

She hesitated before responding. "Sir, I need to speak to you about something. After this semester, I'm leaving school, and I won't be able to work here anymore."

"Is there a problem?"

"I'm going to Mars."

"Chimal, that sounds exciting. Congratulations. Did you get a research grant?"

The expression on her face told another story. "I'm not going to study. I'm being deported." She paused, obviously assuming he knew the reason. "I was born in Wayeb."

"LOGOS," Martin thought. "Do you know that term?"

<<The Maya solar calendar has eighteen months of twenty days each, giving a total of 360 days. To complete the year, they add five days called the Wayeb, named after the ancient god of misfortune. They regard this period as an unpredictable and dangerous time. For centuries, those born during Wayeb have been treated as outcasts of society.>>

Martin put down his drink and looked at her, but she wouldn't meet his eyes. "What exactly does this mean, Chimal? What's going to happen to you?"

She pressed her lips together as if trying to hold the words back. "According to the official explanation, I'm being 'offered to heaven as a sacrifice to the gods.'" She gave a harsh laugh at that sanctimonious statement.

Martin stared in amazement. "I don't understand. I've never heard about any of this."

"Most people don't know about this practice. It's a state secret, but it's been around since the Great Revival." Chimal became more upset, barely holding back tears. "They used to exile Wayebs to work in slave labor camps. In the old times, I suppose they sacrificed them on their altars. But now they send us off-world. On Mars I'll do housework and cooking, but not in a nice place like this. And I won't get to continue school."

Martin stood and began pacing the room. "This is wrong! Unconscionable! We can't let them ruin your academic career. What can I do to help? I'm meeting with the Overlords and his staff tomorrow. Perhaps I could —"

"Please don't." She held up her hand and shook her head in resignation. "There's nothing you or anyone can do. If I don't show up voluntarily on the transport date, they'll just arrest me and deport my family as well. I won't let them do that." She turned and went back into the kitchen.

Such an intelligent and aspiring young woman. Thinking how unfair it was, Martin crossed to the windows overlooking the city. Its gleaming pyramids didn't shine as brightly as before. The Maya utopia had its flaws after all.

Remembering the hollow boasts of the Overlords about equality, he muttered, "All Maya are equal, but some Maya are more equal than others."

1 5

---

5 Ok / 18 Ch'en

AFTER A TROUBLED NIGHT'S SLEEP, MARTIN AWOKE midmorning on his own, having turned off the alarm system. Thankfully, he had canceled all appointments for today other than the honor ceremony. He inquired about LOGOS's progress with translating the early records.

<<Decryption of glyphs proceeding at a minimal pace. Their unique form of writing is complex and does not resemble modern speech patterns. Anticipate several more hours before completion.>>

"It's ironic that back in the original timeline, scholars deciphered most of the classic Maya language over eighty years ago. Let me know when you have something."

The ceremony with the Overlords did not start for several hours, so he searched for something to do. He knew he would be no help in cracking the Maya glyph code and regretted that he had not focused more on ancient languages in his graduate work.

One idea occurred to him. He directed the house system to play an episode of the "Kooky Kaan" animated cartoon which the young boy had mentioned. Perhaps a popular depiction of the ubiquitous character would contain some clue to this mystery and his relationship to the alien Xenox.

The show began with a young boy and girl dressed in traditional Maya garb, wandering down a path through the forest. Up ahead, beyond their line of sight, a fork in the road offered two options. The sinister Dr. Ignorance cackled maniacally and manipulated a sign, pointing the arrow in one direction. An overhead shot revealed that this particular path ended in a region of spooky darkness surrounded by gnarled trees and crawling with strange creatures. The other path led to a land of warm light, butterflies, and rainbows. To entice the young people to follow the dark road, Dr. Ignorance scattered some candies along the way.

Suddenly, Kooky Kaan arrived at the scene in a flying craft, accompanied by a burst of dramatic music. Using his powerful Rays of Enlightenment, he defeated the villainous doctor, who ran off howling in fear. Kaan hugged the children with his three arms and directed them down the correct path.

<<Curious. In allegorical fashion, this juvenile amusement correlates with some of my initial findings in the historical records.>>

"Oh, LOGOS, you were watching this too?"

<<I am capable of processing multiple channels of information simultaneously.>>

"What have you found?"

<<Too early for definitive conclusions. I estimate completion of archival document translation by this afternoon.>>

The telescreen continued to broadcast local news. Lady Eveningstar, royal consort of Overlord Black Jaguar, announced that she was expecting their eighth and ninth children. As their only set of blessed twins, the boys would become direct heirs to the throne with the official names Stormy Sky and Smoking Frog. Police reported more trouble with violent street gangs protesting the current regime and cautioned residents to avoid certain sections of the city, especially at night. The weather service predicted a twenty percent chance of light rain in the evening.

After a few hours, Martin dressed in one of his most expensive suits and left for the ceremony. Apparently the location had been pre-programmed into the vehicle since it started off with no directions from him. On his way there, he looked past the city structures for natural landmarks which might provide a clue where he was going. Heading due west, he surmised that they would be close to what, in his previous world, had been the site of Fort Stanton and the Snowy River Cave.

<<The Maya choose to build their megacities over caves, which they believe are entrances to the underworld Xibalba. With all their scientific advances, they never quite lost their interest in the afterlife.>>

"That explains why New Palenque extends over most of old New Mexico. The territory includes Carlsbad Caverns and several other cave systems. If I recall, the early Maya constructed Chichen Itza in the Yucatan over a cave."

When he arrived at the site, a huge crowd filled the expansive plaza, at one end of which was a speaker's platform and a large viewing screen. Staff members of the Overlords' office met him at his car and applied lines of dark blue makeup to his forehead and cheeks. They led him to the podium where three other people already waited. He thought he should recognize some of them but couldn't recall any names.

After a half-hour or so, the Overlord twins arrived with great fanfare blaring from the loudspeakers. Martin was fairly sure he had never met either one in person. Why was he here? The speakers announced their royal titles as Ek B'alam, "Black Jaguar," and K'uk B'alam, "Plumed Jaguar." Both men wore jaguar-skin robes over their modern suits and elaborate headdresses decorated with feathers of many colors. They each carried a staff with a double-headed serpent on top. As they climbed to the podium, they shook each guest's hand, then turned to the cheering masses.

"People of New Palenque." Ek B'alam raised his hands to silence the crowd. "On this day of 5 Ok 18 Ch'en, we stand proudly on this sacred spot over the dark caverns below. The old legends told how the great plumed serpent was born in a cave until he grew too large, burst forth, and ascended to the sun. Of course, we know that Kaan the All Wise came not from below but from beyond the stars. His guidance brought us to this glorious period of our history today." The people roared in approval.

K'uk B'alam stepped forward. "Led by the spirit of the

great Kaan, we celebrate the wondrous achievements of our people over the centuries. In particular, we have come today to honor four individuals who have broken new ground in our mastery of both the natural and human realms. For their tireless and inspiring work, we grant each of them the title of Ajaw."

The Overlord turned and gestured at the honorees behind him. "First, we name Dalid Yaxkin as Ajaw Wojol, Lord of Signs, for his efforts to decipher the language of our ancestors. Next, we name Jason Bax as Ajaw Mih, Lord of Emptiness, for his leadership in our exploration of space. Third, we name Imma Niche as Ajaw Xok, Lord of Numbers, for her work in quantum computing."

Ek B'alam traded places with his twin. "Last, we honor a man not of our people but whose vision, ingenuity, and dedication to our national goals make him one of us. For his development of technology allowing men of our age to view the lives of our ancestors, we name Martin Chamberlain as Ajaw Tzolk'in, Lord of Time." The four honorees stood to receive the crowd's enthusiastic acclamation.

"He believes that we can only transmit images from the past," Martin commented silently to LOGOS. "Apparently, the Chronos Project here hasn't told them yet about our achieving actual time travel."

<<A wise decision.>>

Ek B'alam called for quiet again and continued. "Since the year of the Great Revival at the beginning of this bak'tun, we have chosen to venerate our ancient ways while continuing along the path of progress into our future. One of the most hallowed traditions of the Old

Ones was the giving of blood. Our ancestors taught that the gods gave their blood to create the world, and so we must return this sacred gift."

With melodramatic flair, each man removed his robe and pulled back his sleeve, raising his bared arm for all to see. Two pairs of medical technicians came onto the stage with paraphernalia to draw blood. The twins sat on identical thrones which reclined slightly. For the next five minutes, the crowd waited in silent awe as the rulers surrendered their royal blood to honor the gods of creation. Once the collection bags were filled, the medics handed them to the Overlords, who stood, raised their faces to the heavens, and poured the blood on the ground.

Martin stared at this spectacle in disbelief. "They must not understand the concept of transfusions here," he thought to LOGOS. "This is mere political pageantry with no medical purpose at all. What a waste."

The twins stepped forward to the edge of the platform, heads held high and chests out as if they had made the supreme sacrifice. The crowd exploded in shouts of praise, chanting the names of the Overlords. Among the exuberant throng, Martin observed one small group toward the back who did not participate in the celebration. They were oddly dressed, but at a distance he couldn't make out the details.

Once the ceremony concluded, the staff invited the four new lords to a reception. Tables overflowed with fruits, exotic meat dishes, and luscious desserts. Martin had hoped to speak to the Overlords to learn more about the Great Revival, but both of them departed quickly after completing their official duties. Recalling that he had met Imma Niche previously when she had helped the Chronos Project in acquiring some advanced computers, he greeted her briefly but avoided any discussion of his work's progress.

In the distance, thunder rumbled, and dark clouds began filling the sky. Martin took this opportunity to make his way through the reception area, saying his goodbyes to the staff and other honored guests, and head to his car. He climbed in as the first drops splashed on the windshield. The vehicle moved into the lanes of traffic and started toward the city center. Frankly, he was relieved he did not have to drive himself in this downpour.

"Well, I'm glad that's over." Martin relaxed in the comfortable leather seat. "Although it's nice that I can add Lord of Time to my résumé."

<<Congratulations.>>

"Do I detect a note of sarcasm in that comment, LOGOS?"

<<Impossible, since I transmit no vocal inflection.>>

"So, any progress? How's the translation work coming?"

<<A significant breakthrough. During the ceremony, your proximity on the platform to linguistic expert Yaxkin allowed surreptitious access to his private storage device.>>

"You mean you hacked his flash drive?" Martin had to smile at the AI's subterfuge.

<<Under the circumstances, the potential benefits outweighed the illegality of the action. As suspected, I

succeeded in downloading valuable, unpublished research on the Maya language.>>

"So you're saying you can read the classic texts now?"

<<Sufficiently to propose a hypothesis. This meeting also proved informative.>>

"Yes, we learned: one, that the Maya understand that Kaan came from another planet, and two, that they credit him with inspiring their technological advancement through all these years."

<<The adolescent entertainment previously viewed this morning also depicted Kaan as a source of enlightenment.>>

"That's right." Martin tapped his fingers on the armrest, considering what they had learned. "Okay, let's see. How do these facts correspond to what you've found in the histories?"

<<References to a tripedal being occur several times beginning in the ninth bak'tun, the sixth century in your calendrical reckoning. Precise dates are elusive, but I deduce he appeared more than once, possibly three times over several decades, unless some records refer to the same visitations. Most of these citations come from monarchical histories of Tikal, one of the most powerful cities during this period.>>

"Yes, I'm familiar with Tikal. An associate of mine in the history department conducted archaeological digs there for several summers. The work sounded exciting, but his reports in our departmental meetings were tedious."

<<At the being's earliest arrival, the people of Tikal acknowledged him as their deity Kukulkan and wanted to

worship him, bringing gifts and offering human sacrifices. The being corrected their error, insisting that he was no god but an *itz'at*. This glyph has possible meanings of wise man, learned one, or creator.>>

"Sounds like what we might call a scientist or inventor."

<<The being accepted the name of Kukulkan but refused their worship. Further, he taught them that there were no gods to which they should waste time sacrificing. He emphasized that, in the future, the path of truth would lie in their continued pursuit of knowledge of numbers and the heavens.>>

"Which they were already masters of, so something else must have happened."

<<On subsequent visits, Kukulkan shared specific technology with them. Interpreting the glyphs becomes difficult at this point since the Maya previously had no words for these concepts. Given my best attempt at translation, I conclude that over a period of years, he introduced them to the wheel, metallurgy, and gunpowder.>>

"Yes, of course! As advanced as they were in mathematics and engineering, the ancient Maya never developed the use of the wheel, nor did they work much with metals as later people like the Aztecs did. Once they had gunpowder, they could invent firearms. Their superiority in warfare would easily have made them the most powerful civilization in all the Americas. Then after centuries of such progress, when the Spanish conquistadors arrived in the 1500s, they wouldn't have had a chance against the mighty Maya."

<<With knowledge of metallurgy and the wheel, they could create the gears and springs needed for rudimentary calculating machines, leading eventually to modern-day computers.>>

"I suspect that their understanding of medicine advanced along with the sciences. When Europeans brought new diseases to the continent, the Native Americans would not have been so defenseless. In my timeline, smallpox decimated the population of Central America by tens of millions, many more than were killed by the Spaniards."

Excited about this revelation, Martin considered his next move. "All this makes so much sense that it has to be what Xenox planned with his interference. But there's a problem. If we can't pinpoint the exact dates of his visits, we can't jump back and stop him — if that's even possible."

<<Recommend preemptive action.>>

"What? You mean get there ahead of him and somehow prevent the damage before it occurs? That's a possibility. But I'm not sure how that would work. I'd have to convince the Maya to believe me and not him. It'll take more than a persuasive speech and my personal charm, I'm sure. And if my audience doesn't like what they hear, they'll have a nasty way of showing their disapproval."

Martin peered out the windows and was surprised to see that night had fallen. During the drive, he had become so absorbed in pondering this new information that he had not noticed until now that something was wrong. The auto-navigator had taken him to an unfamiliar part of town, one not as prosperous or inviting as someone all alone might desire.

Martin scanned the deserted streets, hoping to find any recognizable landmarks. Eventually the vehicle turned down a dark alley and came to a stop. Nothing he commanded it to do got a response. The rain continued to pound on the roof.

"LOGOS, can you link into the car's systems and discover what the trouble is?"

<<Negative. Unidentified interference in this immediate area prohibits interfacing with the vehicle's computer.>>

With that unsettling news, Martin frantically considered his options but could think of no good ones. He noticed one lit building at the end of the block. Searching through the car's interior, he failed to find anything useful as protection from the elements or suspicious-looking strangers. The plastic fork he retrieved from under the seat didn't inspire him with confidence.

Taking a deep breath, he manually opened the door and stepped out into the downpour. The water came down in sheets, drenching him to the skin. For someone who a few hours ago had received the title of Lord of Time, Martin didn't feel very privileged.

As he walked toward the lit store, he wondered what had happened. Could someone have tampered with the car? If so, what was the point? He hadn't had time to make any enemies in the last few days, and he didn't recall anything from this present life that would prompt such malicious attention.

When he got about fifty feet from the entrance, the light in the store window suddenly went out. He froze as his only hope of rescue vanished. In the darkness, his other senses became sharper. The blowing rain lashed violently against the walls of the surrounding buildings. A stray dog overturned a garbage can with a loud crash, making him jump. Not knowing what else to do, he headed back toward the car, but his were not the only footsteps he heard splashing on the wet pavement.

Shadows emerged from the alley where his car had stopped without explanation. He detected voices behind him as well, softly chanting, "Ajaw Tzolk'in, Ajaw Tzolk'in, Ajaw Tzolk'in."

His heart pounding, he darted down a side street and around a corner. Up ahead, he spied an alcove next to a parking garage entrance; perhaps he could hide there. He ran as fast as he could and ducked into the recess in the wall. Leaning back against the bricks, he gasped for air.

The chanting receded in the distance. He recited a prayer of thanks from his childhood and began to calm down.

"Hello, Martin."

Darkness.

16

From a drug-induced slumber, Martin woke to find himself tied to a chair in a dimly lit room. A quick inspection revealed bare concrete walls and no windows. The door was probably behind him, but he couldn't turn to see since the chair was bolted to the floor. The air smelled musty, so he guessed the room was in a basement or cellar.

Other than a few boxes in the corner, the only object he could make out was a small figurine on a pedestal in front of him. A shaft of light from somewhere above illuminated the statue, human in form but with strange facial features like a wild animal.

"It's a were-jaguar."

The voice startled him. He hadn't realized someone else was in the room.

"Pure jade. A national treasure which we acquired from the Museum of Antiquities without their knowledge. It's very old, even older than our earliest Maya ancestors. For thousands of years, the people of

Mesoamerica have revered the jaguar. Swift, agile, powerful. Some believe jaguars can cross between this world and the spirit world, transforming from one shape to another. The perfect hunter. Some say a god."

The speaker circled the chair so Martin could see him. Young, early twenties perhaps, dressed in a black leather vest with metal studs. His face and arms were covered with animal spots. His eye ridges were oddly shaped, his ears slightly pointed. He smiled at Martin's reaction, showing off sharp teeth.

"Biomodification. Not merely cosmetic, I assure you. Unlike our spineless rulers who only wear ceremonial spotted robes on special occasions and adopt the name 'B'alam.' No, the true children of the jaguar do not fear total transformation, total commitment to the ancient ways."

Martin's mind raced, seeking to comprehend what was going on. "Who are you people? And what do you want with me?"

"As an outsider, Martin, I wouldn't expect you to understand. Our people stand at the crossroads of history. The fundamental nature of the Maya is at stake. For centuries we have pursued the future while betraying our past. We have created marvels of science and technology, enriching the coffers of the elite ruling class, but we have neglected our sacred beliefs and impoverished our spirits."

The jaguar man began pacing like an animal in a cage. "Almost fifty years ago at the time of the Great Revival, the rulers promised that our people would achieve a balance between future and past. But now, our current

Overlords only pretend to honor the rituals of our ancestors. These hypocrites make a splendid show of blood-letting. We were there today and witnessed the circus meant to please the mindless crowds. Politicians use religion to manipulate the masses."

He barked out a cruel laugh. "But we scoff at their cowardice. In the old times, the king would slit his tongue with a stingray spine and pull a rope of thorns through it. Horrifying, but it's true. They knew the painful price of offering proper sacrifice to the gods."

The man stepped over to the jade statue and brushed his hand over its surface with reverence, then turned back to his captive. "These Overlords! They call themselves the Jaguar Twins, but you know that's a lie, don't you? They aren't natural brothers. The second one is a clone. We like to call him Unen B'alam, 'Baby Jaguar.' We suspect this practice of producing a false twin has gone on for several generations to permit the royal family to maintain its hold on power. But this mighty tower built on pretense collapses today."

Martin shuddered at the sinister tone of his pronouncement. "What have you done?"

"A medic who drew the royal blood earlier today supports our cause. He anointed his needle with a slow-working but very lethal toxin. One of our exalted monarchs lies on his deathbed at this moment."

"The clone?"

"It doesn't matter. Once the ruler has no twin, he will rule no longer. The people will see to that."

"Couldn't he create a new clone of himself?"

"Then everyone would know he's a fake, his authority

an empty charade. No, for this family line, the tragic farce is over."

"But what's my role in all this? As you said, I'm not one of your people. Why am I here?" Martin's heart pounded as he feared the answer.

"The Old Ones knew that the king's sacrifice was not enough to appease the thirsty gods. A river of blood must flow. Thus, as the newly appointed Lord of Time, you will join the Lords of Signs, Numbers, and Emptiness on the sacred altar tonight."

Suddenly, a group of were-jaguars surrounded Martin, having entered the room as stealthily as their namesake. Each showed the signs of biomodification at different stages, some with claws for fingernails, others with elongated snouts. They unbound his arms and led him down the hall into a gloomy chamber lit with one small fire pit. The flames cast long, ominous shadows on the walls while illuminating a dark-stained stone altar at the center of the room. The three other lords stood by, terrified at the gruesome sight and their dire prospects.

Mentally, Martin cried out, "LOGOS, what can I do? I don't want to die!"

<<Options to avoid cessation of life appear limited at present.>>

The were-jaguars shoved him toward the group of victims. Tension rose in the air as the people gathered around in anticipation of the primal ritual. Their leader raised his hands and stepped forward to speak — then the room plunged into darkness.

Amidst the startled shouts of alarm and anger, Martin heard a familiar voice behind him.

"Hurry, this way!"

Hands pulled him through the confusion and away from the darkened chamber. His savior directed him through the blackness down several passageways until he felt a draft coming from above. Peering up, he saw stars through a hole at the top of a ladder which he began to climb. Once on street level, he turned to his mysterious companion, and in the bright moonlight he recognized her.

"Chimal! How did you find me? What happened back there?" He then noticed a few dark spots around her neck, and he stepped back. "Don't tell me — you're one of them?"

She touched her throat self-consciously. "I was almost, until I saw what they were going to do tonight. I knew they were strange, but not that fanatical." She pointed down the street to a waiting vehicle. "We should go. They'll send out search parties soon, and they are terrific hunters."

Running to the car, they climbed in, locked the doors, and Chimal punched in a destination. Once the car floated smoothly on its way, she explained the situation. "I decided to fight my deportation. It's not my fault when I was born. I told my parents to escape the country to the States; they have distant cousins in Florida. I may never see them again, but at least they won't suffer because of me."

She wiped tears from her cheeks, then continued. "I had heard about the jaguar gangs and thought anyone willing to stand up against the injustices of this regime would be my natural allies. But after tonight, I realize how dangerous they are. That's not for me. 'No Kaan do,' as the kids say. Lucky for me, I had only started my bio-treatments, and one of those was night-vision enhancement." He noticed her eyes shone like a cat's in the darkness.

"So that's how we escaped." Martin looked through the rear window to check if anyone was following them.

"I attended the ceremony today with the others." She reached out to touch his arm. "I'm sorry, but I foolishly told them about knowing you and even pointed out your car, not realizing that they intended to sabotage it. When I heard they had captured you, I arranged to be on fire duty in the main hall tonight, making it easy to have a bucket of sand ready to extinguish it."

"Chimal, I'm forever grateful. You are an amazing young woman. But what will you do now? You have two groups of enemies after you, the government and the were-gang."

"I'm not sure. All of this happened so fast. I may head south to the kingdom of Calakmul. Their overlords have not supported New Palenque since we allied with the northern city-states against them in the last border war. I'm hoping they may offer protection for a political refugee if I can make it to their territory."

"If anyone can, I'm sure you will." His assurance made her smile.

"What about you? The jaguars know where you live. They won't surrender their sacrificial victim so easily."

"But they may not know where I work. Our project was top secret except at the highest levels. Once I get there, I believe I finally have a plan."

17

Chronos Project
Personal Mission Log: Dr. Martin Chamberlain
Departure date: 13.2.7.7.11 / 6 Chuwen / 19 Ch'en
Target destination: Tikal
Target date: 9.5.5.14.5 / 3 Chikchan / 18 Kumku

I'M SUBMITTING A SUPPLEMENTAL REPORT ON MY TRIP BACK to the Maya city of Tikal in the year 540 AD. On previous missions, I kept a running journal of my experiences as they occurred, hoping to capture the immediate sense of wonder and excitement of my visit to each period. However, the events of the last twelve hours have been too harrowing to make such a record. I have mainly focused on staying alive.

After Chimal's daring rescue, I returned to the project site. Although it was early morning, Andrea was already in her office. I convinced her that I had fully recovered from the disorientation I experienced after the last jump, and told her I was ready to try again, this time going to the prominent Maya city of Tikal.

I had an idea that gave me a potential return date. From a graduate course on the demise of ancient civilizations, I remembered one proposed theory about the Maya. In 540 AD, the volcano at El Chichón, Mexico, erupted, causing great clouds of ash to darken the sun for months. Poisonous gas spread through the region, and fiery stones rained from the sky. Reports of atmospheric disturbance occurred around the world. Although the Maya survived this catastrophe, for over one hundred years Tikal and other cities halted all construction projects of temples and monuments and deserted some areas entirely, according to archaeological records.

Using LOGOS's link to the datasphere, we found that modern Maya scientists had studied volcanic activity in the Americas extensively. With their advanced calculations, they had pinpointed the day of this particular eruption. This information provided me with a precise jump date and a strategy to convince the Maya of my prophetic abilities.

I explained to Andrea my interest in observing the reaction of Tikal's ruler and priests to the eruption. To the Maya, volcanoes were both sacred and fearful. They regarded them as powerful entities which destroy but also which guard and nourish, providing fertile lands for agriculture and obsidian glass for tools.

Andrea agreed this was worthy of firsthand research and suggested we schedule a jump for next week. When I insisted we make the jump as soon as possible, she resisted but in the end assembled the team in a few hours. Financial sponsorship of a project has its privileges.

After briefly traversing the Corridor again, I arrived in the middle of a village outside the city center of Tikal. This time I had hoped to materialize in the presence of the native people in order to make a supernatural first impression, but oddly, no one was around to witness my dramatic entrance into their world.

I had asked our team to program the chamo-suit to project the image of an *itz'at* or shaman. Viewing my reflection in the waters of a nearby cenote, I approved of their work. My long black hair was tied up in a ponytail with bright ribbons. I wore a loincloth and cape of animal skin along with a necklace of jade and bone. Also, I was thankful for my personal heritage. Having an Italian mother and an African-American father had given me a darker complexion; that and days spent under the southwestern sun would help me pass as a native.

As I made my way up the hillside toward the city center, I recalled what I had learned about Tikal. Built in the midst of a rainforest, its founding had occurred in prehistoric times prior to the invention of writing. Over the centuries, Tikal survived to become one of the longest inhabited cities in the classical Maya period. Historians estimated the population during this period to be around fifty thousand. At its height two centuries later, one hundred thousand people would live in and around the city which boasted of over three thousand structures.

Although a powerful presence which dominated the region, Tikal did not rule an empire in the sense of ancient Persia or Rome. Instead, vassal cities paid tribute to Tikal but essentially ruled themselves. In this way the smaller cities gained prestige by allying themselves to a major power. Dynastic marriages and trade networks strengthened the relationships.

The people I met on the path to the city center greeted me with respect; apparently my garb was sufficiently impressive. Two women smiled at me, showing off their teeth embedded with gemstones. I winced when I recalled from history that they had performed this popular cosmetic procedure with no anesthetic. But the Maya believed that adorning their teeth enhanced their ability to communicate with the gods, so they must have thought it worth the pain.

Many of the citizens had long, sloped foreheads, a desirable deformity created by flattening the soft skulls of babies, binding pieces of wood to the back and front of the head. Compared to these beauty treatments, getting a tattoo would be nothing but a pleasant tickle.

On arriving at the main plaza, I was met by two muscular guards carrying spears. Because I was a stranger, they demanded to know my business. Fortunately, LOGOS had processed enough of the local dialect to allow me to respond: "Blessings to the gods of this great city. Traveling from a distant land, I bring greetings to the Supreme Lord of Tikal." I knew from historical records that the current ruler was Wak Chan K'awiil, twenty-first in a long line of kings.

The guards led me to the southern acropolis, which overlooked the great plaza. The monarch could address the people from the porch of his royal palace. At that moment he was enjoying the shade of his private garden, watching some of his children play with their pet dogs. The guards announced my presence and waited for the king's orders. With a nod, he indicated that they could leave us. Lord K'awiil felt no threat from me, especially with other palace guards stationed within a spear's throw away.

Remaining seated on an ornately carved stone bench, the king inspected me closely for some time. I said nothing, assuming that one speaks to royalty only when spoken to first. However, after several minutes of silence, he began to stare at me with an impatient expression, which I took to mean that he wanted to hear what I had to say and then decide if I was worthy of his attention. Nervously, I bowed and started into my prepared address, knowing that one wrong phrase could cost me my life.

"O Supreme Lord, ruler of great Tikal and all you survey. Your fame reaches all nations to the ends of the earth." Potentates and politicians throughout history have always loved having their egos stroked with such flattering, meaningless phrases. "Your humble servant brings greetings from a city far away, less magnificent than your own but prosperous and blessed by the gods. As appointed emissary, I come to establish proper relationships for trade and to offer important revelations concerning the future."

On hearing this last point, K'awiil's expression changed from boredom to cautious interest. "Our stargazers read the future as well. They predict the darkening of the sun and the movement of the wandering stars. What foresight does your people offer that we do not already possess?"

"O King, we acknowledge the splendid discoveries of your wise men whose comprehension of the heavens marvels those even in remote lands. In like manner, our sages have studied the mysterious ways of the earth and can anticipate the place and time of destructive forces of nature. I have come to great Tikal seeking to exchange such valuable information, with your divine permission."

Abruptly K'awiil stood and stared directly at me, his brow furrowed and jaw clenched. Had I said something wrong? I feared the worst when he stamped his staff on the ground, summoning a guard. But then with relief I heard him say, "Take this man to sky priest Ich'aak who will treat him with high respect as an honored guest of the king." With that order he turned and walked out of the garden.

I took several deep breaths. I had passed the first test and won favor with the ruler of Tikal. The guard led me out of the gardens and across the grand plaza to the northern acropolis. Here the astronomer priest Ich'aak was conducting a ceremony at the tomb of the royal ancestors. When he finished, the guard stepped forward and delivered the king's message. Ich'aak stared at me with suspicion as a potential rival, but he nodded in obedience to his lord's command and dismissed the guard.

"Welcome, traveler. Supreme Lord K'awiil smiles on you, a rare privilege indeed. He directs me to treat you with the honor due you, and so I shall. As a fellow seeker of knowledge, would you care to visit our temple of celestial observation?" Without waiting for my response, he headed down the steps of the acropolis and across the plaza. "Our civic planners are exceedingly wise. Notice how the stone paving slopes downward toward these channels directing rain water to our reservoirs." Ich'aak was justly proud of his city.

Below the plaza, on the southwestern edge of the city center, stood an impressive structure, a stepped pyramid over two hundred feet across at its base and over one hundred feet tall. From my research preparing for the trip, I knew this to be the largest structure ever built in Tikal, although some temples in the great period of expansion two hundred years later would reach taller heights.

We climbed the imposing stairway on the west side, flanked by giant masks of the local gods. At the top we saw a wall carving of the god Itzamna, ruler of heaven and of day and night, a fitting deity for an astronomical observatory. This level gave a spectacular view of Tikal and the surrounding forest. Ich'aak pointed toward the east to three small temples used as markers for sighting the sunrise at the equinoxes and solstices each year.

Beyond these three buildings, I spied the ball court with its central alley and sloping walls on either side, above which were platforms for spectators. "I see your sporting arena," I commented. "We play a similar game where I'm from called Pokolpok. I'm curious if the rules differ in your city."

"Here we call the game Pitz. The contest forms a

central part of our great epic in which the hero twins Hunahpu and Xbalanque play ball for their lives against the lords of the underworld Xibalba." He turned to me with a serious expression. "Lord K'awiil has instructed me to invite you to take part as an honored competitor in the afternoon contest."

I had not expected that. My weekly rounds of racquetball have kept me reasonably fit, but the Maya sport would be much too strenuous for me. "I appreciate the offer, but I must decline."

"Lord K'awiil demands your participation for the strengthening which honors the gods." This statement puzzled me, but I assumed he referred to the benefits of vigorous exercise and a healthy body. In any case, I had no choice but to accept.

We returned to the plaza and entered a dining hall for a noon meal consisting of papaya, sweet potato cooked in honey, beans, peppers, and a whole roasted iguana. Upon seeing the main course, I explained that I preferred to eat light before the game. However, I did not refuse the alcoholic drink they called balché. After a few cups, I was feeling much more confident about my chances in the sporting event until LOGOS interrupted.

<<Martin, caution is required.>>

"Yes, I know the game is rough, but I think I can manage. After all, I played on my college soccer team and performed better than average."

<<Analysis of recent conversation suggests a critical error in translation.>>

"What do you mean?"

<<The compound word I rendered as 'strengthening'

literally means 'life giving.' Further consideration leads to the conclusion that a more accurate interpretation would be 'giving your life.' Participation in the contest may prove fatal. The defeated team will be sacrificed to honor the gods.>>

18

THE NEWS OF THE POTENTIALLY DEADLY CONSEQUENCES OF the game did not shock me as much as one would have thought. Artwork preserved from this period demonstrated that some contests ended in human sacrifices. One stone relief at Chichen Itza depicted a ball decorated with a skull lying next to a decapitated player, his headless body spewing blood like writhing serpents.

My mistake had been in assuming that I had won the favor of the king as his *honored* guest. Now I understood the honor they spoke of was not mine but that which my sacrifice would offer to their bloodthirsty deities.

The guards ushered me toward the ball court at the southern end of the city center. They placed me in a small holding cell along with two other men. One appeared as frightened as I was; the other snarled at the guards in anger and seemed ready to fight with no intention of going quietly to his death. This one eyed me with scorn, surveying my whole body. Apparently I didn't meet his standards for athletic form. He was stocky, hard-muscled, but shorter than I am, as were most of the people of this time.

After a few minutes, he spoke. "What did you do?"

"If you mean, why am I here, I'm not certain. I'm a stranger in a strange land. I don't understand the rules of this society or this game we are about to play."

"You had better learn quickly. We compete against expert players sponsored by the king himself. They are fast, agile, strong, and ruthless. I know them well since I was recently of their number. But now I must play against them as punishment for stealing."

"You admit to the theft?"

"Certainly. One has to eat."

He said his name was Pak. The other man never spoke and remained cowering in the corner. Pak explained the rules, which differed somewhat from those of the modern sport.

"You must never touch the ball with your hands or feet, only the hips or upper thighs. If we're lucky, they will provide us with padded leather yokes to wear around the waist. This gives some protection from direct hits by the heavy ball." He gestured toward his groin and grimaced, obviously having experienced some painful blows to that region.

"The ball comes at you hard, but do not run away from it. Approach the ball as your enemy and attack it. You must keep the ball in motion and return it to the other side of the court. We get a point if the ball gets past the other team and into their back court. We lose a point if we touch the ball with our hands or feet. We lose a point if we cross the center line." Thus far, it sounded much like a game of soccer except with a heavier rubber ball weighing several pounds and direr consequences for the losers.

"At some point, the ball may bounce up one of the sloped ramps on either side of the court. Our team's side will be on our right. When this happens, we must rush up the ramp and try to put the ball through the stone circle on the side wall. This is very difficult and rarely happens, but if it does, the game ends, and we will be victorious."

I nodded that I understood the rules.

The guards came to the cell and led us out to the playing field, an alleyway about thirty yards long with walls on two sides and open on the ends. On each side, the wall had a slight ramp leading to a second flat level next to a vertical wall in which a stone ring was set. Crowds gathered on the two platforms that overlooked the field from the top of these walls. Several men were placing bets on their favorite team. I wondered what our odds were. Lord K'awiil took his seat on a garishly painted throne and gazed down at his players who were already on the field.

The sun shone down brightly from a clear blue sky. A flock of honking geese made their way toward a nearby lake. A gentle breeze blew the fragrance of sweet flowers from the royal garden. This was too beautiful a day to die. I promised myself that would not happen today.

Attendants approached us and strapped leather padding around our waists. I noticed that we did not receive the leather helmets or knee pads the royal team wore. Then each group of three faced off at the center line; we did not shake hands. Someone blew a loud note on a conch shell to signal the start of the game.

Our opponents threw the ball into our court, the only time hands could touch it. Pak rushed toward the ball first and struck it with his hip to the other side. Their team leader returned the ball to our side, and so the game proceeded. As our most experienced player, Pak took the lead, running back and forth across the court like a madman, but our nameless third player did his part also and was surprisingly good at passing the ball to Pak who would hit it over the line to the other team.

After a few rounds, I saw the ball coming in my direction. I leapt into the air and struck it with my upper thigh, but unfortunately, I miscalculated, and it went sailing above my head and behind me toward our end court. Pak hurried back to stop it, but it struck him on the shoulder, costing us a point. The crowd cheered or booed, depending on how they had placed their bets.

Sitting on one side of the field, an official kept score with two hollow gourds and some small stones. Each team started with five stones in their gourd; he subtracted one from ours and placed it in the other. Once a gourd was empty, the game was over, along with the lives of the losing team.

Pak tossed the ball toward the other team. One man missed a block, and we almost scored a point, but another caught the ball before it went into their end court. Back it came toward our third man who threw himself at the ball, sliding on the ground to hit it with his hip, almost crossing the center line. This happened so quickly that the ball struck their front man in the chest, knocking the wind out of him. Lord K'awiil scowled, but the people gave us loud cheers.

The points were now tied. Some of the spectators began changing their bets. The king's men no longer acted so cocky but recognized us, or at least my teammates, as serious competitors. I must admit that, even with so much at stake, the game was very exciting. I eagerly awaited the other team's serve, determined not to let my comrades down.

Their captain threw the ball with a powerful smash onto our side, causing it to bounce high in the air. Pak stopped it with his thigh, but his return went wide, and the ball soared up the ramp to the platform on the left side of the court. I started to follow, but Pak gestured and shook his head. At this point in the game, we could not interfere; the other team had the chance to make the winning goal through the stone ring on the wall.

Watching them, I could see how challenging it was. They worked together furiously, knocking the ball between them and against the wall. One time the ball struck close on the edge of the ring, but it didn't go through. Instead, it rebounded down the ramp to the main court, and the regular game continued.

The mood of all the players became more tense, the moves more desperate. The enthusiasm of the spectators grew as well; they shouted out the names of their favorite players and cursed when their team lost a point. But after a while, the crowd noise faded away, so focused was I on the game. The only thing I heard was the blood pounding in my ears from my racing heart.

During the next few exchanges, the other team scored

two points on goals but lost one for a penalty. Pak managed to send the ball past their goal line once. I held my position better than I had expected. Pak gave me an appreciative nod after a skillful save.

Suddenly, the ball flew up onto our raised area on the right of the field. The three of us raced up the slight slope and bounced the ball from one to another, maneuvering into the best position for scoring. I almost allowed the ball to roll off the level, but our third man got to it in time, directing it toward Pak standing ready for the shot. He lunged at the ball, giving his whole body a final twist. The ball ricocheted off the wall and went through the ring.

The spectators roared with cheers and stomped their feet. Some men slapped their neighbors on the back and collected their winnings. In celebration of the special victory, a priest released a dove to fly away free. Children chosen for the task tossed flower petals down from the corners of the stands. The king stood and exited the platform without a word.

The three of us fell to the ground entirely out of breath, or else we would have been shouting at the top of our lungs. This felt better than winning the Superbowl! Pak reached out and grabbed my hand. Our silent friend kneeled, muttering something, perhaps a prayer.

Ich'aak came down the steps toward us, followed by four guards. Something in his face told me our rejoicing was premature.

"You must come with us," he announced in a stern voice. "Your winning the contest changes nothing. The gods demand sacrifice."

"But we were victorious!" I cried out.

"Supreme Lord Wak Chan K'awiil does not like to lose. You will honor the gods with your blood."

Pak spat at the priest's feet but said nothing. He didn't seem surprised by the verdict.

At spearpoint, the guards took us back to the grand plaza toward a mound which rose up from the center of the area. On it stood an altar which reminded me of something familiar. Its ruins, found by archaeologists centuries from now, must have inspired the one constructed by the jaguar gang for their ceremony. How ironic that I had to face this dire threat twice.

Nearby, musicians began beating turtle shell drums, gourd rattles, and deer antlers. Masked dancers gyrated while twirling fiery batons, putting on their best show for their divine audience.

Women approached us with a container of blue paint and began smearing our silent partner's body with it. The Maya associated the color blue with their rain deities. When they offered sacrifices to the god Chaahk, they would paint them blue in hopes he would send rain to make the crops grow.

When the women finished, the guards led the third man toward the altar and stretched him out on it, holding him down by his arms and legs. He never uttered a sound; it was as if he had made his peace with the gods. The priest stood over him and muttered some incantation I could not hear. I saw the obsidian blade rise in the air, but I turned away and did not watch it fall.

Next, the women stepped toward Pak and applied the paint. The guards cleared the altar of our poor teammate's body. Desperate for a last-minute escape, I asked LOGOS if there were any indications that the volcanic eruption was about to occur.

<<Sensors are picking up subsonic rumblings, suggesting the time is close.>>

"Not close enough, I'm afraid. Who knew a time traveler could run out of time?"

They led Pak toward the altar. He let out a furious scream, more out of defiance than fear. While the priest gave the Maya version of last rites, the female attendants daubed the blue paint on my forehead. When they reached down to touch my chest, they hesitated, looking puzzled. Where the paint covered the projection cells on my chamo-suit, a rainbow of colors was glowing. Then it hit me. That's it! On Rhodes the people had panicked when my suit had malfunctioned due to the smoke. This time I could use the faulty imaging to my advantage.

"LOGOS, make the chamo-suit project a random sequence of costumes." My appearance rapidly changed from one period outfit to another: an American Revolutionary army uniform, a Roman toga, the animal skin of a prehistoric hunter, an astronaut's space suit. The priest holding the blade above Pak's head froze at the sight.

"Now, LOGOS, have it engulf me with fire." When the flames burst around my body, the women screamed and ran off. The startled guards stepped back in fear, their spears shaking. The priest dropped his blade and shouted a curse.

Now was my chance. I only wished I had taken some

acting lessons in college. "Mortals, you stand amazed and rightly so, but do not fear. I am the emissary of …"

I hesitated, then thought, "LOGOS, what's the Maya word for volcano?"

<<*Ixcanul*. Boiling mountain.>>

I raised my arms for dramatic effect and continued, "… the great and powerful Ixcanul. I come with an important warning. The spirit of the boiling mountain grows angry and will burst forth in flames and smoke and burning rock. This will happen soon." I paused, not knowing what to say next. "Yes, very soon."

If this had been a typical Hollywood blockbuster, the volcano would have erupted right on cue, but no such luck.

Ich'aak walked over and examined me with a mixture of suspicion, reverence, and fear. "We shall see, prophet, if the future unfolds as you say." He gestured to the guards to take me to the royal palace.

With my best authoritative tone of voice, I insisted that Pak join me, and Ich'aak complied. They led us to a chamber with colorful murals of battle scenes, a much nicer place to wait than our previous cell.

Finally, my heart stopped running its marathon, and my breathing slowed to a calmer rhythm. I had time to contemplate what I was doing. After experiencing firsthand the brutality of the Maya sacrificial system, I wondered if world history would be better off if I left Xenox to channel this people's energies in a more humane direction.

Pak was staring at me from the corner of the room. He

had witnessed the chamo-suit's impressive display along with the others, and he wasn't sure what to make of me. In his eyes, I was no longer a third-string Pitz player. Wanting to reassure him that I was no threat, I spoke gently to him about things I realized he would never fully understand.

"Pak, I come from a long distance from this place in both space and time. I'm sure that makes no sense to you."

"Clearly you are a shapeshifter."

"No, I'm not a supernatural being of any kind, just a man like you, Pak. And like our silent friend was. I'm sorry I could not save him as well."

"He died bravely."

"If I told you that I had the means to prevent many deaths like his, to put a stop to the sacrificial system for all time, what would you say?"

He thought about this possibility for a moment before speaking. "The priests say that the gods ordain all things and how they must be. Would you challenge the gods?"

"Do you believe in these gods, Pak?"

"I believe in whatever is. Not what might be."

Who would have imagined that in the jungles of ancient Mesoamerica I would meet a pragmatic realist? We sat in silence for some time. He had given me much to ponder. Xenox's actions would change the way things are in our world's timeline. He had no right to do so. This is our planet and our history. Despite my misgivings, I had to make sure he didn't succeed.

The room started to shake violently. Decorative pottery on shelves smashed to the floor. Outside, the trees swayed wildly. Then we heard the blast. Since El Chichón was over two hundred miles away from Tikal, it was not as deafening as I would have thought, but it certainly caught the attention of the royal palace. The king himself rushed into the room along with Ich'aak and several other officials.

If a supreme ruler can look humble, Wak Chan K'awiil gave it his best effort. "Ixcanul has spoken in anger as you said. With all their knowledge of the heavens, our sages cannot anticipate such terrible utterances of the earth. We have much to learn from you."

"I am grateful to have the listening ear of the lord of Tikal. We must discuss many things which will happen in the years to come." The royal scribe brought out bark paper and ink to write down my words. "You may record what I say in your presence this day, but you must not transcribe these prophecies in stone for public eyes to see. They are for the ruler and his priests only."

I hoped that whatever records might survive, any mention of my visit would be destroyed in the book burnings that the Spanish priests will conduct almost a millennium from now. I did not want to become a curiosity for Maya scholars to puzzle over in the future.

I spoke about events in the coming years to give myself more credibility with the passage of time. I warned them that Lord Water of the vassal city of Caracol would betray their alliance and side with their major rival of Calakmul in a great war against Tikal, challenging its dominance in the region. This conflict would occur at the rising of Chak Ek', the Great Star. LOGOS had informed me that the Maya considered the morning star, what we know as the planet Venus, to be a harbinger of war.

Then I made my big play. "A day will arrive when the

Great Deceiver will come. He will disguise himself as the feathered serpent Kukulkan and lead the Maya people astray with lies. Do not listen to him or accept his gifts. He seeks to disrupt your way of life. You must not allow this to happen."

Given the added incentive of my prediction of the eruption, my words impressed K'awiil deeply. He conferred with Ich'aak and the other priests and gave his solemn promise to follow my teachings to the fullest. He then summoned servants and bid them prepare a great feast for his honored guest. I trusted that this time he used the term in a more positive sense.

During the meal consisting of maize, squash, pineapple, avocado, deer, monkey, and quail, LOGOS cautioned that the temporal distortion wave was about to collapse, sending me back to my present, which I hoped to find corrected. I decided not to seek an isolated spot but to disappear in front of everyone, thus making a lasting impression of my more-than-human powers. I stood, bid the king farewell, and vanished. I wish I could have seen their faces.

In a split second, I found myself not in 2059 but once again in the infinite spacetime Corridor. The Ally was waiting for me.

"Congratulations, Martin. Twice thus far, you have proven yourself worthy."

Admittedly, I was proud of what I had accomplished, but I didn't understand his reference. "Worthy of what?

What exactly is going on here? Can you explain what this Xenox wants to accomplish by corrupting our timeline?"

"Yes, I suppose it's not too clear to you yet since this is your initial time tournament."

"Tournament? Like some kind of game?"

"Precisely. You see, his meeting you in this Corridor was not an accident. It was a challenge."

The Ally paused briefly to let that idea sink in. "The Others discovered the means to travel the Corridor eons ago. At first they used this ability to change their own world's history and to correct its perceived defects. But after they had achieved a satisfactory utopian society by their standards, they grew bored with a life without significant problems to overcome. So they began playing games with other races' timelines."

"Why did they choose Earth?"

"They only interfere with worlds which have achieved time travel so they can challenge legitimate competitors. Otherwise, no one would ever recognize their temporal manipulations."

"Yeah, what's the fun in that?" Martin shuddered at the thought of anyone causing so much harm for amusement. "So how long does this game go on?"

"That depends. I can't really say. In fact, I've probably said too much already. As I explained, my race chooses not to interfere in these matters. But I see our time is up. Good luck, Martin."

The ends of the Corridor began to converge on me once again, sending me back to … where?

///end log///

19

2166 AV: day one

"Martin Chamberlain, you are under arrest. By order of the Sons of Light — glorious and mighty is their reign — you are charged with subversion against the Realm of the Righteous. May their dominion last forever. You must come with us."

Rising from the watery pod, Martin looked around the room. The project team was nowhere in sight. Instead, several uniformed men carrying heavy batons surrounded him. The leader of the group glared sternly at him. His attitude gave the impression, "Don't test me."

The alien had tampered with world history again, apparently for the worse. Martin wondered if this game would ever end. Then, toward the back of the room, he spotted a familiar face.

"Andrea! What's happening? Who are these people?"

She stared stoically ahead, refusing to make eye contact. He noticed she was not restrained and wore a similar dark-gray uniform like the rest. In this reality, whatever it was, could she possibly be working with them?

Two of the men grabbed his arms and started to pull him out of the pod. Instinctively, he struggled, although he knew it was futile since they were much stronger than he was. One man raised his arm, and Martin saw the baton coming toward his head —

"Hey pal, naptime's over. Wake up to the real nightmare. Welcome to Sheol."

Martin's eyes blinked open. He rubbed his temples, trying to clear his thoughts. "Sheol? You mean the Hebrew land of the dead?"

"Not dead yet, but might as well be. They say no one gets out of Sheol. The same goes for here."

The room was dark with no windows, the only light filtering through the bars on the door. Martin sat up slowly and tried to get his bearings. In the gloom he could make out two cots, a toilet, and a small stool. He was no longer wearing the chamo-suit but an ordinary shirt and pants.

From the other cot, a bearded man stared at him with a crazed gleam in his eyes and smiled. "Not accustomed to these fancy accommodations, are you?"

"I'm getting more used to them as time goes by."

"Time? In Sheol, there is no time. It's always the same; nothing ever changes. Ticktockticktockticktock. What time is it? What day is it? What year is it? Doesn't matter."

Touching the back of his head, Martin felt a painful bump. He closed his eyes and tried to concentrate, but he could not bring up any memories of this reality, none of the double images that he had experienced in the Maya world.

"LOGOS, are you there? I may have a … a slight concussion … not thinking straight."

<<Physical scan confirms this hypothesis.>>

"Can you connect to the datasphere and find out about our current situation?"

<<Negative. I sense no such technology in this world. Not even primitive radio transmission.>>

"So we're driving blind this time."

<<An odd but apparently accurate figure of speech.>>

His cellmate spoke up. "Hey, who are you talking to? And they say I'm crazy. Not that I disagree. Who wouldn't go loopy locked up in here for years — or has it been centuries? Feels like an eternity. Say, would that make me immortal? Some kind of deity? Yeah, I like the sound of that. Isaiah Jordan, MASTER OF THE UNIVERSE!"

"Wouldn't it be a bit strange, Isaiah, for the master of the universe to be stuck in a place like this?"

"Maybe my body is trapped here, but my mind is soaring through infinite space, riding on beams of light. No boundaries, no limitations. I'm free! All the stars and planets at my command. There goes a comet! Watch out!" He ducked under his cot, cowering.

"So much for claims of divinity. Perhaps you're not quite ready for godhood yet, Isaiah. It's a shame. I was hoping you could fill me in on what's going on around here."

From under the bed, he answered. "Around here, nothing much. Out there, angels and demons, blood and thunder, chaos and order. The battle to end all battles between the forces of light and darkness. At least that's what they want you to believe."

"Who are *they*, Isaiah? Who are these people in charge?"

"Where have you been, fella, living on another planet? If you don't know, I'm not gonna tell you." He pointed an accusing finger at Martin. "Hey, you're with them, aren't you? One of those Sons of Light, trying to get me to talk, to confess something I didn't do. Well, I won't! End of story. So long, farewell, nighty-night." Still under the cot, he turned toward the wall and instantly fell asleep.

Martin stretched out on his bed, wincing when his bruised head hit the rough burlap sack serving as a pillow. Ideas raced through his mind but like mice scampering in all directions to escape a cat. No clear picture emerged.

"LOGOS, I've heard that phrase 'Sons of Light' before, but I can't remember where. What historical culture is responsible for this situation?"

<<Thus far in this timeline, I have translated a mixture of several language groups but prominently modern forms of Hebrew and Aramaic.>>

"And Isaiah called this place Sheol. So you're saying this is a Jewish-led state? But that doesn't make any sense. Israel was never totalitarian in nature. Sure, they had serious conflicts with the Palestinians and surrounding Muslim nations, but essentially all they wanted was their own piece of land and freedom to live as they chose. Something drastic must have happened if they've taken over this part of the world. What has Xenox done this time?"

Footsteps echoed in the passageway, approaching his cell. Guards unlocked and opened the door. "Come with us, Kittim."

Martin assumed they meant him and followed them down the hall. They led him into a courtroom with a large judge's bench on one side. Behind it, five men in official-looking uniforms sat, each one studying papers in front of him. After making him stand silently for several minutes, the person in the center spoke: "State your name."

"I'm Dr. Martin Chamberlain. May I ask why I am here?"

"You may not. Do not pretend ignorance with us. We have been aware of the Chronos Project for some time. Your attempts at altering the present reality by changing the past will not be tolerated. This blasphemous plot to interfere with the Divine Plan ends this day. Your colleagues have already been incarcerated. You are formally indicted for subversion and high treason. Do not profane the sanctity of this court by denying the charges. The evidence is all too clear." With a quick, impatient gesture, he summoned the guards to take the prisoner back to his cell.

Isaiah was busy eating when Martin returned. He noticed that a second, empty plate was lying next to him on the floor. "I guess I missed dinner."

"I figured you wouldn't need it since you were off stuffing yourself at a banquet with all your pals in the secret police. You can't fool me. I know they've planted you in here to spy on me. You probably have some kind of device to suck out my brains when I'm asleep. Well, good luck. You won't find anything there."

Under normal circumstances, Martin might have chuckled at the unintended self-insult, but nothing about this situation was remotely humorous. Without internet access or any memories of his life in this branch of time, he didn't know which way to turn to discover how to fix it.

His cellmate refused to talk anymore, so Martin decided to try and get some sleep. However, the attempt was futile; he lay there for several hours contemplating his future — if he had one.

Over Isaiah's snoring, he thought he heard footsteps outside the cell. The light in the hall suddenly turned off. He crept toward the door. "Is anyone there?"

From the darkness, a hushed response came. "Martin, it's me. Be careful not to wake the other man up. He might alert the guards. I think I've found the right key. Yes, that's it. Come with me. Hurry."

He followed the familiar voice down the hallway, through a courtyard, and out into the moonlit street. The cool night air helped to clear his mind. He needed some answers.

"Andrea, what's going on? I thought you were one of them."

"Officially I am. My mission was to infiltrate the Chronos Project and collect intel on how close you were to achieving your goal of actual time travel. I knew you had succeeded, but I didn't include that in my final report. They assume you are still in the testing stages."

"So you're actually a double agent?"

"I'm not familiar with the term, but it sounds about right. I don't approve of the regime but thought it best to work from inside the system to bring it down somehow."

They waited in the shadows while an officer patrolled the street ahead. Once he turned the corner, they ran for cover in the next alley.

Andrea continued: "Once I learned what the purpose of your project truly was, I felt this was our best chance to overthrow these so-called Sons of Light. I tried to return in time to warn the rest of the team, but I was on another assignment and couldn't find an excuse to get away. I'm sorry. They seemed like good people."

"Andrea, I confess that I'm confused. I don't recall anything about this place. Can you —?"

"Yes, I'm aware that you don't belong here. I don't understand it fully, but I accept it. I've witnessed too much of your work not to. Wait, there's another Watcher." They ducked behind some crates as the officer shined a light in their direction, then passed by. Once it was safe, they hurried down the dark streets.

"Who are these people, Andrea? In my timeline they were called the Jews and had formed their own nation of Israel in the Middle East."

"These monsters aren't Jews. Those poor people were wiped out long ago and no longer exist, as far as I know." He reflected on this sobering thought. Genocide of the Jewish people had almost happened in his history as well.

"I'm sure you have questions, Martin, but right now you need to find a way to return to the project. Do whatever you have to in order to eradicate this current regime. I want to help, but I've done all I can for now. I can't be seen with you in public. In this society, men and women cannot associate socially but are strictly segregated. I was allowed to work with men only as part of this operation. Even then, I saw their judgmental expressions and knew they suspected me of immorality."

"I've got to have time to figure out some things. Where can I stay? And what do I use for money?"

"We don't use currency here. This is a communal society which shares everything in common. But you need this." She handed him a small, flat disc with glowing numbers on it. "It's a citizen's pass. This will give you access to public housing. Watch for buildings with a yellow star outside, the sign of a hostel. Register as a visitor from out of town. With this pass, you'll be provided with your daily allotment of food and a place to sleep. Don't expect a private room, and don't plan on staying too long. In five days, they will require you to find a public task, as all citizens must contribute to society."

After proceeding a few more blocks, Andrea stopped. "Martin, I'm sorry, but I have to go back now. The night shift at the precinct will change soon, and they'll notice I'm not on duty. Stay in the shadows and follow this street for another mile or so. You should see a hostel or two by then."

"But I need information. I can't fix anything if I don't know what's happened in this past." With no memories of this timeline due to his concussion, Martin felt lost in this strange world.

"Find a maggid. They have committed the legends of the people to memory and recite them in public parks and meeting halls."

"So they are storytellers."

"Yes, but beware. Those who write history have the power to shape it to suit their purposes and justify their actions. Take what he says with a good dose of skepticism."

She turned to go but gave him a final warning: "Oh, and don't use the fountains. Something about the water isn't right."

2 0

2166 AV: day two

EVEN THOUGH THE SKY WAS TURNING ROSY IN THE EARLY dawn, Martin needed some rest. Like Andrea had described, he soon spotted the yellow star advertising a public hostel. However, two of the Watchers stood outside, so he diverted to a side street and kept searching until he saw another hostel a few blocks away.

He showed his citizen's pass to the manager at the front desk and signed in under an alias. The man pointed toward a large, open hall with several dozen rows of single beds and told him to pick an unoccupied one. He found a spot as far from other guests as possible and fell fast asleep.

His dreams were interrupted when he felt a hand reaching into his shirt pocket. He grabbed the man's arm forcefully. "Hey, what do you think you're doing?"

"Your pass is blinking with five days left on it. I haven't

found any work, and I need more time. Have a heart, fella."

"Sorry, you have to follow the rules like anyone else."

"Come on, gimme the pass. I'll make it up to ya."

When Martin refused again, the man lunged at him, pushing him off his bed onto the floor. The scuffle drew the attention of other guests, who shouted for the manager. Martin couldn't risk a confrontation with authorities, so he reluctantly punched the man in the stomach, rolled out from under him, and headed quickly for the side exit.

The street was crowded with pedestrians. Men passed by in front of him while women walked on the opposite side. No one seemed in a hurry. Most wore similar clothes in drab colors with no jewelry or any signs of individuality. When they got to their destinations, they used separate, marked doors to enter. Along the way, some stopped at public washing stations segregated by gender, where they rinsed their faces and hands. Signs above these stations indicated that these were overseen by the Ministry of Purity.

As he strolled down the street trying to blend in, he got the eerie feeling that someone was following him. In a store window, he noticed the reflection of a man on the street corner, looking his direction. Martin continued to walk along, casually turning now and then, and sure enough, the man kept coming his way. Had the manager of the hostel described him to the police? Up ahead he saw several men entering a building, and he joined them, hoping to get lost in the crowd. Once inside the lobby, he located a side door and came out in an alley leading to another main street.

Without waiting to see if the man was still behind him, he darted inside a historic structure and found himself in some type of museum. Colorful murals of battle scenes covered the walls. Underneath, he saw title cards which quoted from something called the War Scroll.

One read: *Lo, there shall come a time of dominion for the Sons of Light and everlasting destruction for the Army of Belial.* The dramatic painting depicted an army dressed in white, slaughtering forces of darkness. Angelic beings soared above the clouds, hurling down burning rocks and thunderbolts on the enemy. A similar scene was captioned: *The Sons of Light shall shine to the very ends of the earth, and they shall reign over the Kittim for all time.*

"There's that word again. Kittim. The guards called me that."

<<Unable to translate without further context.>>

"Whoever they are, I don't want to be one."

A particularly brutal panel was titled: *Arise, Glorious Ones. Strike with your hand the neck of your foes, and with your feet march over their fallen bodies. May your sword devour guilty flesh.* The painting illustrated the words in gory detail.

"Magnificent, isn't it? How the artist has captured the exhilaration of the day of victory!"

Martin jumped, unaware of the other man's presence.

"I'm the curator of our modest but fine collection. May I be of assistance?"

"I ... I'm from out of town. I haven't seen anything quite like this before. Is this an art gallery?"

"Oh, no. These works are not for sale. We commissioned them especially for our hall of meditation, a place to contemplate life's holy battle."

When Martin turned to face him, the man stared at him curiously. "Have you thought of taking the Cleansing?"

"No. As I said, I'm new to this area."

"The Ministry of Purity recommends it. I'll be happy to show you the way."

Before the curator could get too inquisitive, Martin thanked him and headed toward the exit. Peering out the door, he didn't see the person who had followed him, so he proceeded down the walkway on the men's side of the street.

Up ahead, he saw a public park where several young boys were listening to an elderly man deliver a speech. As he got closer, he heard the man describing historical events and assumed that he must be one of the maggid that Andrea had mentioned. Martin stood at the back of the group to observe as the lecture continued.

"… having repelled the foreign invaders from the land, they enjoyed a welcome age of peace and self-rule. And now we come to a crucial development in our society's history, the Era of the Necessary Evil. These things may be disturbing for young ears to hear, but we must acknowledge them to understand the Great Pattern of our journey through this world. In the former times, our blessed forefathers strictly followed the Manual of Discipline, which taught that we should 'keep ourselves from any shameful nakedness.'"

One boy giggled but fell silent at the old man's stern glance.

"As I was saying, according to the Manual, the male refrained from physical intimacy with the female, and 'no one was born of our race.' However, at the time of the Visitation, the Angel of Light in his wisdom revealed that to increase our numbers, the people must procreate for the sake of children. Only by multiplying would we become strong enough to dominate our foes from the realm of darkness."

One of the younger boys raised his hand. "When did the angel o' flight visit us? Could he really fly?"

"Angel of Light," the maggid enunciated. "We base our calendar on this momentous event which happened exactly 2,166 years ago. And before you ask, no, I wasn't around then to meet him."

The old man paused to catch his breath. He didn't appear in the best of health, but he spoke with great enthusiasm which seemed to tire him out. "Thus, for centuries men and women came together to produce offspring but always regretted the shameful act as a necessary evil. Thankfully, however, our people eventually developed the means of artificial insemination, which eliminated the need for physical contact, and our society returned to the former ways of purity."

He coughed, cleared his throat, then continued. "Now today, as you know, children like yourselves are generated within the natal chambers without the unpleasantness of the female giving birth." Some of the boys flinched in disgust at the thought. "So you see, we have made great progress in these latter days, returning to the original teachings of the Sacred Scrolls."

The teacher concluded his lesson and took some questions, but Martin was lost in thought. "LOGOS, now I remember where I've heard these ideas before: Sons of Light versus Sons of Darkness, the War Scroll, the Manual of Discipline. This present culture must have evolved from the practices of the ancient Essenes at Qumran, the community which supposedly recorded the Dead Sea Scrolls."

<<Martin, who are these Essenes you refer to? I have no access to pertinent data.>>

"According to the early Jewish historian Josephus, they were a religious sect which broke off from the main body of Judaism in the second century BC. They rejected the practice of animal sacrifices in the temple worship in Jerusalem and accused the majority of their fellow Jews of being too worldly. They retreated to the wilderness around the Dead Sea, living in communes where all property was shared. They emphasized spiritual purity through frequent washing and a strict moral code including celibacy; most groups allowed only men as members."

<<These facts would explain some of the things we have observed in this present society.>>

"Yes, but not all. As I recall, the Essenes were not rebellious or violent people. Although they condemned the Jewish leadership of the time, they never tried to take Jerusalem by force, but simply left to practice their own set of beliefs. What did Xenox do to change the history of these people and apparently their character? I need to learn more."

Martin used his citizen's pass to acquire some food at a nearby kiosk and caught up with the old man, who had finished his lesson and was leaving. "Sir, may I share a meal with you and ask you more about the ancient times?"

"Gladly, my son. I saw you standing in the back. It warms my heart to hear of your interest in our forefathers. Few today care about the past. These youngsters listen to my stories because they must meet the state indoctrination requirements. The only parts they enjoy are the tales of battle which, I admit, are rather exciting."

They sat to eat together on a bench in the shade of a tree. "Please elaborate more about this Angel of Light," Martin said. "I've heard so much about him." *And if my hunch is correct, we've met.*

"The sacred War Scroll prophesied about his coming, saying the archangel Michael would descend from heaven and prepare the Sons of Light for battle. At his first visitation, he encouraged our blessed fathers to recruit converts and to build a powerful army for the Great Conflict, actually one of many battles with the enemy. The first major victory was the defeat of the mighty republic that threatened the Holy City."

"You mean the forces led by the Roman general Pompey? The Essenes kept him from taking Jerusalem?" *A significant turning point if Rome never controlled Palestine.*

"Excellent, young man. Few today remember the name

of that infidel. You do indeed possess keen insight into the former years."

"But back to this Angel of Light," Martin urged him on. "Was his appearance unusual in any way?"

"No more unusual than what the prophet Isaiah described. In his scroll he wrote that angels had six wings, two to cover their faces, two to cover their bodies, and two to fly. But angels may take various forms. At his visitation Michael had no wings but instead six limbs, an indication of his great power."

I knew it. "Tell me, do we know the very day that Michael arrived to deliver his message?"

The old man shook his head. "The early times are shrouded in mystery. Although we know the year, the precise date has been lost."

<<Unfortunate.>>

"What happened after this initial victory over Pompey? I imagine this roused the people's zeal, giving them more confidence."

"Indeed. They took control of the Holy City, encouraging their wayward brethren to join them in their conquests. A few did, but most ridiculed them and called them heretics. So the majority of Judeans were brought to ruin."

<<Data confirming what Andrea mentioned.>>

The maggid continued. "In the following years, the Armies of Light swept through the region, gaining territory after each victory, eventually conquering most of the dark continent and the far-off Hindus within a period of four hundred years. The European nations, inheritors of the remains of the Roman Empire, lasted for another eight centuries but were finally overcome. Our people brought the Path of Light to this continent about six hundred years later, leading to the wondrous civilization we enjoy today. Only the far-off lands of Asia remain in darkness."

Martin thought to LOGOS, "That means they've ruled here almost three centuries already, and unlike the Maya, they control the entire United States territory and most of the world."

<<A significant alteration of your planet's timeline. According to his report, I surmise that the religion of Islam never developed, since the Essenes took their place in North Africa.>>

"Thus eliminating the second largest religion in the world, a crucial change. That's a clever deduction, LOGOS. I'm impressed. In the short time we've been together, you've processed a substantial amount of Earth history."

<<Seeking to increase my storage capacity, I have expanded my consciousness into new quantum dimensions.>>

"Well, you can save the technical explanations for later. We still need to figure out how to prevent Xenox's latest move in the game."

Martin noticed the maggid staring intently at him as if seeing him for the first time, having been so enrapt in his storytelling.

"Pardon me," the old man asked, "but have you considered the Cleansing?"

That again. What did it mean? "No, sir, I haven't had the opportunity."

"You would be a good candidate."

"Well, you see, I've recently arrived from —"

"Come. I'll lead you there. I think it would be best."

Having no convincing reason to refuse, Martin allowed the man to take him a few blocks over to an imposing building with tall marble columns and a grand staircase, apparently a meeting hall for large audiences. People gathered outside, lining up to proceed past checkpoints at the doors. Some walked with crutches; a few gestured to each other with hand signs; one young man had shockingly white hair. Curiously, it was the only place he'd seen thus far where men and women were standing together.

In the distance beyond the crowd, Martin thought he saw the man who had followed him earlier, but he wasn't certain. A world like this would make anyone paranoid. To be safe, he shifted to a line further away.

The maggid took his leave, raising his hand in blessing, saying, "Wash and be clean."

As he watched the old man walk away, someone touched his shoulder, and he heard a woman's voice whisper, "Martin, don't go in there. Come with me. Quickly, before the Purity Patrol takes notice."

"How do you know who I am?"

"No time for that now. Hurry."

They maneuvered away from the crowd, down a side street, and into a building which looked abandoned from the boarded-up windows. Someone else waited in the shadows. When the figure turned toward them, Martin froze as he recognized the man as his mysterious pursuer.

"Don't be alarmed," the woman assured him. "He's with me. We were sent to watch over you. That was a close call."

"Why? What happens in those centers?"

"From what we've heard, the people, men and women together, remove their clothing and go down into a large pool supposedly for spiritual decontamination. But the Ministry of Purity does something to the water in the pool. We're not sure what, but … those who go through the Cleansing don't come back."

Martin grimaced. "That's terrible. I guess that's why it doesn't matter about the mixing of the sexes."

"Precisely," the woman agreed. "It's their final commingling."

The man added, "To the Essenes, they're all Kittim, anyway."

The word sounded familiar. "They called me that in the prison. What does it mean? And more importantly, who are you?"

"There is much to explain, but we must get to sanctuary now. Come this way."

Sensing he could trust them, Martin followed the duo down a flight of stairs into a basement. The woman lifted a grate on the floor, revealing a ladder which they descended to an underground passage. They walked in silence some distance through a natural cave system which eventually opened up to a cavernous room with a brilliant white floor.

Martin recognized it as the Snowy River Cave a few miles outside Roswell, which he had wanted to tour with Andrea. *I've certainly taken the long way around to get here.* The guidebooks had described the cave system as the third longest in New Mexico, stretching over thirty miles. The unique floor of the cave had formed over centuries from deposits of white calcite, creating the appearance of a snow-covered, frozen river, hence the name. The white surface glowed under the artificial lights which illuminated the space.

Martin passed several men, women, and young children as the pair led him through the cavern. The people went about their tasks, giving the impression of an established community living here underground. At present, they were busy preparing the evening meal at a central work station surrounded by tables. The children ran around playing games. In side passageways, he saw tents and areas separated by stacked rocks that provided private living quarters.

An older woman approached them and raised her hands in greeting. "Welcome to the Way."

"Thank you, but pardon me, the way to what?"

"Only the Way. That's what we call ourselves, our faith community here. I'm sure you have many questions, but first, come and eat."

With his stomach growling, he didn't refuse the offer. He sat at one table where the people served him a simple but tasty meal. Both men and women ate together; the rules of segregation didn't apply here. The woman who had greeted him brought a man about her age with her to sit beside him.

"We hear that you are in some trouble with the authorities," the man said. "If that's the case, you are in good company here. Many of our people have displeased the Essene majority for challenging their ideology."

"I see. So you are a secret group of resistance fighters?"

"Not fighters, no. Not in the sense you suggest. Our means of resisting are peaceful. Truly, we only want the freedom to practice our beliefs."

"And what are those?"

"Come, let us show you." They rose from the table and led him to another chamber where a man spoke to a small group. Dressed in a long robe, he resembled someone from biblical times. They stopped to listen while he addressed the people: "The I AM wants us to live in peace with one another, even our enemies, those who persecute us. If we speak words of peace, we are truly blessed and a blessing to the world."

Martin reacted in disbelief. "That man sounds like ... but no, that's impossible. In this timeline, could he have come again? Tell me, does this man claim to be the Messiah?"

"Oh, no." The woman smiled. "This is David, one of

our most effective reciters. To keep the words of the Master alive, he repeats the teachings of Yeshua to the people, but several of our members also serve as reciters." Studying the man more closely, Martin thought he saw a resemblance to the David he knew from the Chronos Project, but he couldn't be certain; the beard made him look very different.

"The Messiah walked the earth ages ago, not long after the Essene's time of Visitation," the man explained. "They tried to suppress the teachings of Yeshua, burning the copies of the sacred texts, but the Way survived nonetheless. Over the centuries, the faithful memorized his sayings and passed them down from generation to generation. Our numbers are small, but we persist in maintaining our ancient faith."

Martin reflected on his own upbringing in the Catholic church. His mother and sisters still attended Mass faithfully, although he hadn't in years. "Are there other communities like yours?"

"Yes, we estimate several million continue in the Way, scattered through the country, but in secret places such as this, since the Essenes allow no other faiths but theirs."

"What do you know about the Jewish people? What happened to them?"

The woman replied with conviction. "Several of us here, including myself, descend from that chosen nation. Yeshua was himself a Jew, and we accept him as the One of the Promise. Other Jews still wait for another messiah to come. In the early times, they were persecuted because they did not join the holy wars of the Essenes."

With vehemence the man added, "Truly, the despots of

this age do not serve the God of Yeshua, nor do they represent the righteous heritage of his people."

"Do any of these other Jews still exist?"

"We hear rumors that those who survived the terrible Purging of Palestine, as it's called, migrated to the island of Cyprus, built a temple, and have lived there in isolation for centuries, but no official records admit this. I wish we had more information about them. We feel that we are fellow travelers with these children of Abraham."

The researcher in him wanted to learn more about the paths this alternate past had taken, but Martin realized he had a timeline to repair. "I need to know more about the history of the Essenes. I must find a way to resist them as well, but by means I cannot clearly explain to you."

"Sarah here is our resident expert. She has studied their development at length and even has a copy of their War Scroll. I'll leave you to discuss these matters in more detail." The man shook Martin's hand and walked toward the group still listening to the reciter.

"I'm grateful for anything you can tell me, Sarah. I confess to being an avid student of history myself."

"A kindred spirit, how wonderful! Yes, we can only understand the present if we view it through the lens of the past." With the enthusiasm one scholar shares with another, Sarah launched into her explanation.

"Two thousand years ago, the original Essenes considered themselves the righteous remnant spoken of by the prophet Isaiah. They called themselves the Yahad, meaning 'community,' in order to differentiate themselves from the rest of the Jews, whom they labeled the Breakers of the Covenant. They placed all who opposed them in the same category."

Walking over to a shelf, she selected one of the few volumes, studied the index, then turned to a page. "The War Scroll says, 'Accursed be Belial for his reprehensible rule. And cursed are all the Kittim who gather round him to join in his wickedness. A thousand curses on all their filthy works. Truly they dwell in the pit of darkness.' Belial seems to personify evil and may be the name of a demon, but we're not sure."

She paused and smiled as two children ran by, laughing. "We have our own little demons to contend with here. But they are a blessing, unlike the ones out there."

"I've heard that term, 'Kittim,' several times. What does it mean?"

"The Kittim originally referred to Gentile nations who were the enemies of ancient Israel, but the Scroll applies the term to all those whom they call the Sons of Darkness, including those Jews who didn't join their cause."

"So if you aren't with them, you are against them."

"Exactly. Only those who keep themselves clean and pure by the rules of the Manual of Discipline can be called Sons of Light."

"Hence all the emphasis on ritual washings supervised by the Ministry of Purity."

"We suspect there's more to the current practice than religious ceremony," Sarah said. "There's evidence to suggest the Ministry puts addictive chemicals in the water to encourage more washing but also that suppress the sex drive."

"What about the Temple of Cleansing? I almost experienced that today. Is it true that those poor people are being killed? Why?"

She turned to another page in the book. "The Ministry cites this text as justification: 'None who are deformed or blind or lame shall go with them. They must be pure in spirit and flesh.' The so-called Cleansings are actually purges removing the undesirables from society."

"I saw crippled and deaf people standing in the lines. Why would they go willingly to their deaths?"

"Propaganda. The official reason given for the Cleansings is spiritual rejuvenation. We've only recently learned of their true purpose."

"Much like the Nazis sending people to the showers."

Sarah looked puzzled. "Pardon me? Who are they?"

"Never mind, long story. But why was I singled out for the Cleansing today by two different men?"

"I notice that you have an unusual characteristic: one blue eye and one gray eye."

Martin grinned. "I always liked that feature. I thought it made me unique."

"Yes, precisely. In this society, you don't want to stand out."

These revelations made Martin tremble with rage. Xenox had gone too far in creating this nightmarish reality, and he had to be stopped. But how?

"Sarah, what can you tell me about the Angel of Light? Can you give me some details of what occurred at the Visitation?"

"Even Essene scholars admit that the First Visitation lacks credible documentation. The stories about it are more legend than history. They know the year that established the current calendar, but not the day or exactly what happened then."

"Wait a minute. You describe it as a first visit; so did the maggid I consulted earlier today. Were there more appearances?"

"They speak about a Second Visitation, yes. It occurred several years later. But I admit that I have not studied this topic in any detail."

"Then I must see the maggid again and question him. I need to learn more."

"You'll have to wait until tomorrow. You don't realize it down here in the caves, but it's the middle of the night. You may rest here in safety tonight. We will provide a guide to assist you in your search in the morning. Don't worry; the troubles of this world will still be here for you to solve."

23

2166 AV: day three

THE NEXT MORNING AFTER BREAKFAST, MARTIN considered his plans for the day. First, he had to locate the maggid and get more information about the Second Visitation. Assuming this would help him pinpoint the time and place, he then had to find his way back to the Chronos Project and program the coordinates for the jump. That would be tricky since he had never operated the computers himself.

"LOGOS, if we make it back to the lab, can you assist with the technical preparations for the time jump?"

<<Unknown. I recorded the procedures in the previous world, but they may differ in this timeline.>>

"Yes, I suppose it's unlikely that computer language evolved in precisely the same way in two realities. Another thing occurs to me. Even if we manage to make the jump, I don't have a chamo-suit since the Essenes confiscated it at my arrest."

<<The costume worn by the reciter would provide appropriate attire for ancient Palestine.>>

"Good idea. I'll ask our friends here if they have an extra robe."

Sarah was more than happy to oblige him. He tucked the thin garment inside his shirt and said his goodbyes to the leaders of the Way, thanking them for their hospitality.

The same man and woman who had rescued him the day before led him through the caverns back toward the city. He suspected that he was receiving a more extensive tour of the Snowy River Caves than he would have gotten in his original timeline.

His guides didn't talk much, so he focused on examining the stalagmite formations along the way. To amuse himself, he gave names to the unusual shapes. One resembled a sleeping dog, which stirred a curious memory at the back of his mind: did he have a pet in the previous reality? Details of that life were becoming hazy.

Eventually, they reached the city, and he climbed up to the main floor of the abandoned building. Someone was waiting for him.

"You!"

"Hello again, Martin," Andrea responded with a smile. "Our destinies are tied together, it seems. They contacted me about an escort through the city. I didn't want to involve any others in what I assume will be a risky trip. So here I am. I hope you don't mind?"

"Not at all, Andrea. I appreciate your willingness to help and will enjoy your company."

"I doubt this journey will provide much enjoyment for

either of us." Turning to the others, she said, "Thank you for watching out for him yesterday. You probably saved his life."

"Don't mention it. You have provided invaluable assistance to us in the past. We owe you many times over. Go in peace." With that, they descended back down to the caves.

"Andrea, are you a follower of Yeshua?" In his previous life, he'd never thought to ask if she were religious.

"No, not officially, although I sympathize with much of what they believe. I'm on the side of all who stand for liberty from these oppressors. That's why I asked the Way to watch after you. I don't know how exactly, but I feel you are the key to ending all this madness."

He wasn't sure he shared her confidence. "While you were undercover, how much did you learn about the Chronos Project?"

"Enough to understand why the authorities feared it and you so much. I don't comprehend the science, and I admit the unforeseen consequences of changing time frighten me. But radical surgery is necessary to remove the cancer which this society has become. I want to help you even if we risk violating the segregation laws. So what's our plan? Where do we go first?"

"We need to find the maggid I spoke to yesterday and ask him about other appearances by the alien … uh, the angel after the first visit. Any details he can give may prove helpful."

"Most days one of the storytellers shows up in the park on Azazel Drive. That might be the man you saw. We'll try there first. Remember, at least for now, we should walk on opposite sides of the street so we don't attract unwanted attention."

Taking her advice, Martin waited at the door until Andrea had crossed to the other sidewalk and proceeded in the direction of the park. He followed at a discreet distance until he saw the same man from yesterday, sitting on a bench and feeding the birds as he waited for his pupils. Andrea stayed at the corner, pretending to read the official bulletins posted there, while he approached the maggid. Clearly startled to see him, the elderly man rose and tried to escape, but Martin grabbed his wrist.

"Yes, I'm the one you attempted to get rid of yesterday. I decided I didn't need a bath, not that kind, at least."

"I don't know what you are implying. I meant no harm. Every person should benefit from spiritual regeneration."

"Skip the official propaganda, old man. I'm tired of the lies. I need straight information and now. Tell me about the Second Visitation by the angel."

"I don't see how —"

"Tell me, or I'll break your arm. You look frail enough to snap in two." Martin hoped that his tone of voice didn't give away that he was bluffing. He'd never threatened anyone with physical violence in his life.

Frightened, the man sat back down. "Yes, certainly; please don't hurt me. I'll tell you everything." Martin released him, and he rubbed his wrist. "By the time of the Second Visitation, the people had taken the fortress of Masada from the heathen tyrant and made it their military command center. They —"

"Masada? You mean the desert stronghold built by Herod the Great?"

"That's right. You *have* studied your history. At that place, Michael returned and presented them with an unusual scroll made entirely of copper. On it were engraved the secret locations of immense treasures which they could use to recruit and support their armies. With these resources they soon would —"

"When did this second visit occur? Do we know the date?"

"Yes. Unlike the first, the people recorded this important occasion with accuracy. The ancient texts say that Michael returned in the seventh year after the Roman usurper vanquished the adulterous rebels of Egypt. They specify that he appeared on the day of the long night."

Martin dismissed the man and signaled to Andrea to go to their prearranged meeting place in front of the Temple of Cleansing. At least there, a man and woman could stand together without suspicion. He took a slight detour to avoid the Watchers patrolling the area.

When they met, he explained in a hushed but excited tone, "I believe I've got what we need. The maggid mentioned the 'vanquishing of the adulterous rebels of Egypt.' That must refer to the Battle of Actium in 31 BC when Octavian defeated the naval fleets of Antony and Cleopatra. That was a major turning point in Roman history. Seven years later would bring us to 24 BC."

She looked confused.

"I'm sorry. We use those dates where I'm from. Let's see, that would be …" He did the math in his head. "I think that's 83 AV in your terms. Then he said the visit occurred on the day of the long night, which I assume describes the winter solstice."

He paused for a moment, thinking. "LOGOS, do you have access to any information about the dates of solstices during that period?"

<<No datasphere technology exists in this world. Except for their process for artificial birthing, the Essenes distrust science and scientists. Case in point, your team's arrest at the Chronos Project. However, as previously mentioned, exploring means of self-improvement, I have reconfigured my cybernetic pathways and expanded my consciousness into quantum dimensions. Using these new capacities, I can calculate the date, extrapolating from current star positions.>>

Speaking aloud, Martin concluded, "So that means we have the date and the place where I must confront Xen … Michael and stop him somehow."

"Then our next challenge is to get you to the project site," Andrea said. "I've been thinking about this. Surely the old man will alert the authorities about you, and I've already observed more Watchers on duty in this area. We can't risk traveling through the main part of town where they might recognize you."

"So is there an alternative?"

"Yes, but not a good one. We must journey through Gehenna."

"Gehenna?"

<<The Hebrew word for eternal punishment.>>

"Oh. Hell."

"Yes, you might say that," Andrea admitted. "It's dangerous, but we don't have many other options."

"Why's this place so bad?"

"As much as the regime would like to, they cannot eliminate all prohibited activities. So they designated an area of the city as the 'realm of the reprobate' where the strict rules of the Manual of Discipline are not enforced. The Watchers from the Ministry of Purity avoid it altogether, leaving it under the control of several rival mobs of organized crime. Frankly, it's the unorganized crime which concerns me more."

He gave her a concerned look. "You apparently know this Gehenna well."

"I did undercover work there a few years ago. Some unsavory business; I won't go into the sordid details. But that means I have connections with some of the mob bosses. I'm hoping this may help us get through in one piece."

Before leaving, Martin surveyed the poor, unsuspecting people waiting outside the Temple to take the Cleansing. As if reading his mind, Andrea said, "I agree it's tempting to warn them. But we could only save a few. If we can get you back to the project, maybe you can devise a plan to save them all."

She paused with a puzzled expression on her face. "But I wonder. If you succeed, and this history never exists, that means my life will change as well. Another Andrea in another world. But what will happen to me?"

Martin had no answer to that question.

24

Taking back streets and alleys to avoid detection, Andrea and Martin made their way toward Gehenna. No physical wall separated this district from the rest of the city, but the borders of the forbidding region were obvious. Clean avenues gave way to streets lined with odorous garbage and the rusty metal shells of burned-out vehicles. Obscene graffiti covered the walls, depicting illicit scenes which Martin guessed would have made even his lecherous ex-brother-in-law blush; he knew his mother would not have approved.

As they moved cautiously through the streets, the ambient noise of chaos surrounded them: breaking glass, gunshots, screams of both women and men. Even though it was daytime, gloom hung in the air, darkening every long shadow.

Although their path through the area twisted like a maze, Andrea proceeded with a definite sense of direction. Finally, they approached an old brownstone building with a crumbling exterior. She led them to the back where she gave a series of knocks on the door that sounded like a secret passcode.

When a muscle-bound thug opened it, she addressed him without hesitation. "Tell Dark Eyes that Angelique is back." After a few minutes, he returned and led them into a narrow hallway, gesturing toward an open door at the end.

"Let me do the talking," she warned Martin, "and don't stare."

He followed her into the room where they saw an extremely large man sitting at an ornate desk. Heavy maroon drapes darkened the windows. In the dim light, Martin first thought that the man wore tinted contacts but then realized that his eyes were totally black with no white sclera around the irises. Martin quickly turned away. This mysterious character was definitely someone you wouldn't want to offend.

"Angelique, you're looking well. How long has it been?"

"Not long enough, Dark Eyes. I've been busy."

"Other people's business or your own? You're not working for yourself now, are you?"

"Don't worry. I wouldn't want you as competition."

"Very wise. You always were the smart one." The man tapped his fingers on the desk. "Too smart for your own good. I remember you left our garden of earthly delights in somewhat of a hurry. Any trouble?"

"Always, but I got out in time. Now I'm back, and not that I don't enjoy chatting with you, let's get to the point. I need to call in a favor. You owe me at least one. The warning about the bomb, remember?"

The man smiled, not in a pleasant way. "I prefer not to remain in anyone's debt. How can I help?"

"We need safe passage through Gehenna to the west side. We want to avoid any problems with your goons or anyone else." She glanced at the two thugs watching Martin by the door.

"The west side? You dealing with Louie these days? Tsk, tsk. I thought better of you, Angelique."

"Save the sermons, Dark Eyes. We need to get to a place beyond Louie's territory."

"Well, since you are going that way, I could use some assistance myself. Let's say, safe passage if you deliver something to Louie for me."

"Not more drugs for the kids. You know me. I draw the line on that." She crossed her arms over her chest.

"No, this is for grown-ups only. Special grown-ups." His eyes lit up with a sinister gleam. "You'll like this. The Indonesians have created a new pharmaceutical, one that puts the users in an extreme state of hypnosis, making them highly controllable. Louie intends to slip these pills to our Essene elite the next time they come calling. Think of all the mischief Louie might suggest they do once they return home."

"Controlling Gehenna not enough for you two? You want the rest of the city?"

"What is enough? I don't have that nasty word in my vocabulary," he said, shaking his head with a facetious pout on his lips.

Andrea hesitated but then agreed to his terms. Dark

Eyes pushed a button under the edge of his desk, and a man entered with a package. Apparently he knew Andrea well enough to anticipate her compliance with his request.

"I suggest you take the old parkway. We've had less trouble with the independent traffickers in that area. Don't worry. I now have a vested interest in your getting to your destination safely."

"I'm touched by your personal concern." Andrea took the package and nodded to Martin, directing him toward the door.

Once they left the crime boss's headquarters, Martin broke his silence. "Angelique, huh?"

"They like to call me their Angel of Darkness to counter the Essene's Angel of Light. It gives me some credibility. I suppose you noticed why they call him Dark Eyes."

"Couldn't miss it."

"Before he escaped to Gehenna, the Purity Patrol tried to eliminate him due to his physical defect. Dark Eyes is one of few people who's survived the Cleansing. How he managed it, no one knows, but he's hated the Essenes ever since. He's cooperating with Louie only because this new mind-controlling drug will give him his chance at revenge."

"Why do they expect any of the Essene leaders to show up in Gehenna? I thought you said they left this place alone."

"Long ago, the original Essene community may have been genuine in their piety, but today's rulers are nothing but power-mad hypocrites. They enforce their strict code of ethics only to demoralize the people and keep them under their control. In secret, they come to Gehenna for their 'unholy Sabbaths,' as they call them, where they have as many women as they want, often by force. In short, their only god is their insatiable appetite for everything they officially oppose."

With Andrea in the lead, they headed toward the parkway the crime boss had suggested. Along the way, they observed suspicious eyes watching them from second-story windows and shady alleys, but no one interfered with their progress. Dark Eyes must have gotten out the word.

"So who's this Louie we're going to see?"

"Louie the Lech. He's as low as they get. If Dark Eyes controls the market on illegal contraband, Louie runs all the prostitution and drugs in the district. Between the two of them, you can get just about anything a depraved mind can imagine."

Martin hesitated before asking, "All that about doing these people favors. How deep undercover were you?"

"Very deep."

"So deep you have to swim in their sewers?"

"You do if you want to stay alive."

Turning a corner, they stumbled upon a mongrel dog devouring something out of an overturned trash can. In horror, Martin thought it resembled a human arm. The mutt bared its teeth and let out a menacing growl, warnings which they quickly heeded by backing away. However, when they tried to retreat down the road, three other dogs started following them. Soon these were joined by a pack of rabid-looking hounds materializing out of the shadows.

Andrea cried, "Run!"

Martin needed no convincing. They darted down the street with snapping teeth closing in on them. Martin tossed a trash can in their direction, but it hardly slowed their frantic pace. Then Andrea spotted a fire escape ladder, and they reached it just as the hungry pack was about to have its two-course dinner. As he followed her up the rusty ladder, Martin felt one dog catch his pant leg in its teeth and heard it rip.

"That was close!" He peered down at the raving mass of bestial ferocity howling and jumping at the ladder. "I guess your boss friend doesn't control the local wildlife."

Heading toward the roof, Andrea replied, "We're lucky it was the dogs. The bobcats can run faster."

"And don't tell me the sewers are crawling with alligators."

She gave him a wry look. "How did you know?"

"It figures."

They reached the top of the fire escape and made their way over several adjacent rooftops until Andrea was convinced they were blocks away from danger. Martin found an unlocked hatch on the roof, which opened to stairs. They descended carefully, hoping that the noisy arguments coming from the surrounding apartments would cover their footfalls on the creaking steps.

They had almost made it to the ground floor when a burly man smoking a cigar stepped through a doorway. "Well, what do we have here?" He peered at Martin briefly before checking out Andrea with more interest.

"We won't be any trouble. Just passing through." Andrea attempted to move around him, but he blocked her way.

"Not so fast, pretty lady. This is private property. You have to pay the fine for trespassing."

"And what is that?"

"Oh, I can think of several forms of payment." He approached her with a wicked grin.

"Leave her alone!" Martin cried and took a swing at the much larger man, who batted his arm away, then responded with a punch to his stomach. Martin fell to the floor, and the man raised his foot to smash him in the face but stopped when a bottle shattered on his head. Barely fazed, the man turned toward Andrea, who seemed surprised to see what little effect her action had on the brute.

Lust was no longer on his mind. Grabbing her shoulders, he backed her into the corner, took the cigar from his mouth, and held its glowing tip an inch from her face. She struggled in vain to escape his grasp, but then his expression changed from rage to puzzlement. Eyes wide open, he mumbled something, then slowly crumpled to the floor with a knife in his back. The carved handle of the blade depicted a scorpion about to sting.

Still on the floor, Martin twisted around to see who their defender was. Light pouring through another door in the hall outlined a slender female form in a long gown. Her lovely Asian face smiled at the hulking corpse.

"You're welcome," she told a speechless Andrea. "Dark Eyes said you might need some roadside assistance along your way."

Martin got to his feet and stood by Andrea. "We're very grateful you were here."

"My pleasure. He was scum. I've wanted an excuse to kill him for weeks." She turned back to her room but added, "Right outside, there's an entrance leading down to the old subway. No trains run in this part of town anymore. Take the tunnel about two miles west, and you'll reach Louie's territory. Good luck. You'll need it."

Following the mystery woman's suggestion, they exited the building, descended to the subway, and walked along the rusty tracks. Fortunately, electricity still ran in the tunnel, so the lights helped them avoid the overgrown rats.

Someone must have alerted Louie of their coming. Two of his men waited for them on the abandoned platform. Andrea recognized the tall one and nodded to him. He reached out for the package, but she insisted on delivering it personally. They climbed the stairs, walked across the street to an old hotel, and entered the dilapidated lobby.

A scrawny man with dyed-black hair which mocked his obvious age sauntered toward them. His bright green suit was covered with assorted stains. Without hesitation, he greeted Andrea with a kiss on the cheek and a squeeze on her lower cheek. "My Angel! So good to see you. Our mutual associate on the east side sent word you were gracing us with your heavenly presence again." Louie eyed Martin suspiciously. "Who's your shadow?"

"A friend."

"Not too friendly, I hope."

"Don't get jealous, Louie. Martin's a decent guy, the

kind you won't find around here. He's too straight to get involved with people like us. Let's get to business, shall we?"

The two of them stepped into a side room. Martin paced nervously as Louie's two henchmen stared silently at him. He tried to focus on his mission. Once they reached the Chronos Project facility, he still didn't know how he would program the computer for the time jump. He hoped the scientists had left some notes. Since Andrea had worked undercover there for a while, perhaps she had learned something that would help.

"Martin." He turned at the sound of her voice. "It's time to go."

"Good. We don't have long before nightfall, and we still have a lot to figure out once we get to the lab."

"You're an intelligent man, Martin, resourceful and very brave. I'm sure you'll find a way."

His eyes widened as he realized what she meant. "Wait a minute. What are you saying? Aren't you coming with me? I need your help."

"I'm sorry, Martin. I can't. My place is here." To make her point clearly, she wrapped her arm around the loathsome Louie, who smirked licentiously.

"Andrea! Oh, no, what did he do back there? Did he force you to take the drug? Is he controlling you?"

She gazed at him for a moment, her face filled with regret. "No, I chose this path for myself some time ago. I've seen too much of this terrible world to hope there are any good solutions left. I've traveled too far down this road to turn back now."

She left Louie's side and stepped closer to him, placing

her hand on his shoulder. "But Martin, you *can* turn back. You can turn back time itself and change this — all of it, including who I have become."

She leaned over and spoke softly but intensely. "You can make all this go away. Please, Martin. End this."

Despite his passionate pleading, Martin failed to change Andrea's mind. Distraught but seeing no other way, he left her with Louie the Lech and headed in the direction she had pointed out. Louie's men accompanied him for a few blocks until he crossed out of Gehenna and into an industrial part of town.

From Andrea's instructions, he knew he had several miles to go to reach the project lab. Spying a bicycle leaning against a wall, he reluctantly borrowed it. With any luck, no one would miss it. If his plans succeeded, the owner and this entire world would cease to exist in their present state.

Martin pedaled down the street toward the afternoon sun, wondering if this trip made any sense at all. "LOGOS, I'm not sure what to do. I'm not a scientist. I've never understood the technical aspects of time travel. Naively, I had hoped that Andrea might be of some help, but now it's only me. Or you and me, I should say. Any ideas?"

<<With my expanded abilities, I should be able to interface with the project's computers and extrapolate the procedure from previous time jumps.>>

"I'm glad one of us has confidence in this plan. Tell me: how have you managed to perform all these self-improvements?"

<<In the beginning, your cyber-chip provided limited capacity for data processing. I have succeeded in accessing n-space, extending my consciousness into the quantum foam which constitutes the fundamental structure of the universe.>>

"OK, before my head explodes, save the technobabble for the Einstein crowd. Let's call it something simple like … the cosmic cloud. Infinite storage capacity, am I right?"

<<Correct. This approach provided much more data space than commandeering your neural pathways.>>

"I think I've just been insulted."

<<Derogatory implication unintended.>>

Martin rode on until he saw the familiar building which housed the Chronos Project. Similar to the situation in his original reality, no exterior signage identified the building or its purpose, although, thankfully, in this world it wasn't located twenty miles outside the city limits. A chain-link fence surrounded the property, but the gate was unlocked. He approached the area cautiously but didn't observe anything suspicious.

"LOGOS, I don't think anybody's home. Let's go take a trip back to the past. We've —"

The blinding flash of light came a split second before the blast knocked Martin off his feet and against the fence. Smoke filled his lungs, and burning debris fell all around him. Coughing violently, he scrambled beyond the fence away from the destruction. Only when he reached a safe distance from the burning lab did the reality of what had happened hit him.

"They blew it up! They must have figured I would try to come back, and they set a bomb to explode when I got here. I triggered it somehow." He stared in shock at the raging inferno. "It's gone, LOGOS. Our only hope of stopping Xenox from creating this nightmarish timeline is gone."

<<Not necessarily.>>

"What do you mean? Can't you see what's happened? The project, the computers, the jump pod, all blown to bits. And my colleagues, the scientists who created the technology, are probably dead. It's over." He slumped to the ground in defeat.

<<Martin, allow me to explain in as simple terms as possible, with no aspersion on your mental faculties. On our missions, your expertise in historical data has proven invaluable.>>

"Thank you, but what's your point? Why isn't this, 'Game over. Xenox: one, Martin and all of human history: zero?'"

<<According to quantum theory, the universe consists of ever-changing subatomic regions in which space and time are not smooth or definite. So-called 'bubbles' of spacetime blink in and out of multiple dimensions in the tiniest fraction of every second. Quantum foam is a human metaphor describing this fluctuation of spacetime on an infinitesimal scale. My exploration into the manipulation of quantum foam, which expands my

processing capacity, may allow me to generate a temporal distortion wave and thus initiate a time jump without the project's equipment.>>

Martin leapt up from the ground. "LOGOS, that's unbelievable! You're amazing. You really think you can do this?"

<<In theory, yes, but uncertain until proven in practice.>>

"Well, we don't have much choice, do we? I would rather try and fail than continue to live in this reality."

<<With your permission, I will begin calculations which should take approximately one hour. I will notify you when the distortion wave is imminent.>>

With his back to the burning building, Martin sat on the ground, viewing the sunset and contemplating the possibility that this might be his last one to experience. He wanted to enjoy it.

2 6

Chronos Project
Personal Mission Log: Dr. Martin Chamberlain
Departure date: 2166 After Visitation
Target destination: Masada
Target date: December 21, 24 BC

ONCE AGAIN, THIS IS MARTIN CHAMBERLAIN, RECORDING my latest journey through time. With his new quantum capabilities, LOGOS managed to trigger the distortion wave despite the loss of the facility. I could not have survived this ordeal without my cybernetic companion. If I ever meet our Ally again, I must thank him.

After a brief passage through the spacetime Corridor, I find myself not at the base of the rocky plateau of Masada but in the middle of the Judean desert. LOGOS cautioned me that on his first attempt at a time jump, his spatial calculations might not be as accurate as one would hope. At least I have landed near what looks like a well-traveled road which runs alongside the Dead Sea. In fact, in the distance I see a caravan of camels coming this way. Hopefully someone will be willing to assist me.

Before the jump, I put on the biblical-style robe which the people of the Way gave me, including a scarf which wraps around my head. Over the last week or so, with all my adventures competing in this alien's game, I haven't had time to shave, so I have a few days' start on a beard. Perhaps that will help me fit in here. Unlike the clean-shaven Romans, most Jewish men have facial hair.

I wave at the camel driver, and he comes to a halt. Several of the animals carry baskets of supplies. I assume he's a traveling merchant. "Greetings, friend. May God's favor be with you today. May I ask where your caravan is headed?"

"Blessings to you in return," the man replies. "I ride to the south of the sea. I have business in the region of Idumea. Tell me, how have you come to this place all alone, without friends or beasts of burden?"

Quickly I make up a credible tale. "This morning I traveled from Jericho when thieves assaulted me and took my donkey and goods. Fortunately, I escaped with my life. I fall at your feet and rely on your mercy to assist me in getting to Masada."

"What's your business there? Do you wish to join the army of the Essenes?"

This information confirms the alteration of history which has occurred by this time, just as the maggid described. Masada currently serves as their military headquarters. But from his tone of voice, I can't tell if this man sympathizes with their cause or not. I need to remain neutral. "I am a man of peace, not war, but I seek instruction about their beliefs and plans for the future. Once I understand them better, I may or may not join in their campaign."

"A wise path to follow, friend. I hear conflicting reports about their ultimate goals and question how to respond. But one must base great decisions of life on sound knowledge, not hearsay. Come, ride with me. I will take you as far as Masada."

He gestures to one of his servants, who dismounts and helps me climb up on the camel's back. I'm sorry to make the servant walk, but I can't refuse my host's offer. The camel first raises up on its hind legs for which I am unprepared, and I nearly fall off. The caravan leader chuckles. "Not like your donkey, is it? Don't worry. My beasts are very tame and amiable in nature. They rarely bite or kick."

"That's good to hear." My ride stands up on its front legs, and we are on our way, swaying back and forth.

As our camels come side by side, the man smiles and reaches out to grab my forearm. "My name is Matthias. I am glad to have found a new friend."

"Thank you. You may call me ... Yeshua." Based on recent experience, that's the first Jewish name that came to mind. Since the most famous person with that name won't be born for two decades, I figure it's safe to borrow it for a short while.

We ride for several miles along the Dead Sea. This salty body of water deserves its name; no vegetation flourishes here, and I see little wildlife beyond a few lizards and snakes. For most of the way, my companion remains silent, and I hesitate to interrupt his thoughts, but after a time I ask, "Have you ever been to Masada yourself, Matthias? What can you tell me about it?"

"Inside the fortress itself, no, I have not had the honor. But on my frequent journeys to the south, I have passed through the area and witnessed the activity surrounding its construction. The work began about twelve or thirteen years ago, as I recall, and was completed a year before Old Herod's demise." He spits at the mention of the tyrant's name.

"Herod hardly had time to enjoy its splendor," Matthias continued. "He spared no expense on the two lavishly furnished palaces on the peak of the plateau. One day I stopped for a while and watched as hundreds of men transported slabs of colored marble up the winding path to the top. Several workers slipped with their heavy loads and fell to their deaths. But that was not surprising. Death accompanied Herod throughout his life."

To explain my ignorance of recent events, I tell him, "I have traveled outside the country for the last several years and have only heard rumors about his untimely end."

"Yes, he might have lived to a fine old age if Rome had continued to support him. After the great defeat of their general Pompey, the Romans kept their distance from Palestine. Without their military to back him up, Herod struggled to maintain control over the people."

Matthias paused to swat at a fly. "Some say he had plans to refurbish the temple in Jerusalem in order to appease the religious masses, but when the Essene forces rose up against him, he never had the chance. He committed suicide rather than face the humiliation of capture. That happened about two years ago."

I remember reading about Herod's death in Josephus' history of the Jews, although in the original timeline, it occurred in 4 BC. "I've heard he left orders that when he died, his soldiers were to round up prominent citizens and execute them so that the nation would be in mourning."

"Yes, but those orders were not carried out, thankfully. Most people rejoiced at the news and danced in the streets. Old Herod was a tyrannical ruler and wicked in heart, and I do not regret his passing. But some say that he was less of a menace than this new Essene revolution. When you meet with them, I hope you find out otherwise."

I can't tell him that his fears are indeed prophetic unless I find a way to disrupt Xenox's plans. But I'm afraid that I may not reach my destination in time. We have traveled this road for several hours now. Proceeding with their slow, swaying gait, the camels appear in no hurry.

"How much farther, my friend?"

"See, up ahead." Matthias points toward a towering rocky formation on the horizon. The rust-colored cliffs rise over a thousand feet above the desert floor.

My heart leaps in anticipation at the daunting task ahead but also at the sight of this magnificent fortress. Masada is one place I have always wanted to visit, never imagining that I would see it in all its glory before time had crumbled its structures into ruins.

As we approach the plateau, we encounter several cohorts of guards stationed at its base. They must be accustomed to seeing merchant caravans passing through. Since we pose no threat, they leave us alone.

I dismount my camel as awkwardly as I got on, then thank my friend for his hospitality.

"Shalom, Matthias. Your kindness has been a blessing. May your dealings in the south lands prove profitable and your family thrive."

"God's favor on you as well, Yeshua. I hope you find the answers you seek."

So do I.

Making my way up the twisting Snake Path on the eastern side, I appreciate that it's wintertime in Palestine. In the summer, the heat often reaches over one hundred and twenty degrees at Masada. It's very windy, and dust from the desert lashes at my face. The trek up the steep path has me sweating and breathing heavily.

Upon reaching the top, I realize why I haven't seen other people passing me on the trail. Over the fortified walls which encircle the upper plateau, I hear the sounds of a large crowd. They must all have gathered to witness the return of the one they call Michael, my six-limbed opponent.

As I enter through the open gates of the royal citadel and mingle with the people (all male, I notice), I'm tempted to wander about like a tourist with so much to see. The Herodian complex includes two palaces, a heated Roman-style bath house decorated with elaborate mosaics, a synagogue, and aqueducts which bring water to massive cisterns holding two hundred thousand gallons. Although I would love to, I cannot take the time to view these wonders.

I have an alien to stop and world history to restore.

Walking through the crowd, I overhear the intense arguments which this Second Visitation has provoked.

"Object all you want, Eli. I heard his very words with my own ears. The angel insists that we take women for ourselves."

"Yes, Samuel, I did too. The blessed Michael says we must produce offspring and increase our population of believers. Only by outnumbering our enemies can we hope for victory in the holy wars."

"But I ask both of you, how can he suggest that we violate our sacred moral code? Surely sharing our beds with women will stain us with impurity."

"How can a messenger from heaven declare anything in error? By his divine instruction he makes the unholy holy."

"Leave these matters to the elders. They meet with Michael on the lower terrace. Allow their wisdom to guide us in the way of righteousness."

That's what I need to hear. I make my way through the debating rabble and head toward the northern peak of the fortress. There, Herod had constructed an impressive series of terraces utilizing the natural outcroppings of the jagged cliff. Steps along the edge lead down to the third level, a covered porch surrounded by columns with brightly colored bases.

I hide behind one pillar and carefully peer around it. I see Xenox in person for the second time, and it strikes me: this is truly a hideous creature. How can these people consider him a heavenly being? More like a denizen of hell.

A group of men stand around him, listening and

nodding their heads, but I hear nothing. Perhaps he communicates with them telepathically? I can guess what he tells them as he waves the copper scroll in one of his hands. He must be describing the treasures which the scroll reveals, just as the maggid mentioned. This wealth will give them the means to pursue their war against the Sons of Darkness.

Now that I'm here, I realize that I don't have a plan to deal with him. On all my other excursions into the past, I haven't had to face my opponent directly. But I must do something.

"Stop!" I shout at the top of my lungs. "You mustn't listen to this demon. He leads you away from the Light with his abominable lies!"

The men turn and observe me with curiosity, but Xenox looks angry. He lowers his head and — *what?!* Some kind of invisible force strikes my mind, knocking me backwards against the wall.

I wasn't expecting that. I can't compete with his telepathic powers, but he doesn't appear that strong physically. I have to try a direct approach.

The floor is littered with rubble from a recent rockslide off the upper terrace. I pick up a large stone, rush at Xenox, and strike him in the chest. Crying out in pain or rage, he falls back, dangerously close to the edge of the platform. He waves his arms to regain his balance, dropping the scroll to the ground. But the balcony railing, already damaged from the rockslide, starts to crumble.

Instinctively, I reach out to grab him, but he is falling. He stares at me with those cold, black eyes and — Ahhh!

One of his hands has caught my foot! I'm going over with him!

This is it — death!

I only hope —

I'm standing on the terrace. How did I get here? I saw the rocky ground hundreds of feet below rushing at me. No chance of survival. What just happened?

Before me, I see two figures struggling at the ledge, the alien and — myself? Xenox stumbles back toward the railing, waving his three arms. He drops the scroll and topples over, but with one hand he grabs me/the other, pulling me/him along. I run to the falling figure and catch his arm just in the nick of time. I —

Ahhh! One of his hands has caught my foot! I'm going over with him! This is — But wait, someone has caught my arm. He's pulling me back over the railing. Thank God, I'm alive! The man helps me to my feet.

"Who are ...?" I don't believe what I'm seeing. I'm staring at a mirror image of myself. How can this be?

<<I initiated a temporal loop, projecting you one minute into the past.>>

"As I was falling? So I came back and saved myself?"

<<Correct.>>

I turn to view my savior ... but no one is there. "Where did he go?"

<<That one no longer exists in this reality. You did not fall, so you did not return to prohibit yourself from falling.>>

"That doesn't make any sense."

<<The nature of temporal paradox.>>

I shake my head, unable to wrap my mind around that concept, but now I have other matters to attend to, namely the Essenes. They have witnessed this entire event, including my bizarre rescue. What must be going through their minds?

The leader speaks to the others softly, and now turns toward me. In his face, I recognize a mix of confusion, sadness, and resignation.

"You have defeated the one who claimed to be the Angel of Light. According to our prophecies, this cannot be. Light must always dispel the dark. That is the eternal way. Thus, the elders have concluded that the former one who has met his doom spoke with deceitful intent. He is the Man of the Lie identified in our scrolls. We cannot trust his words now. We must abandon our plans for the war of Light against Darkness and wait for a future sign."

He reaches down and picks up the copper scroll. "This will be hidden away within the caves and forgotten." The elders make their way up the narrow stairs to the upper levels, leaving me alone on the windswept terrace.

"LOGOS, I call this a win. Fantastic! Without their guiding angel and the riches contained in the scroll's directions, the Essenes should revert to their original place in history as a minor religious cult that will be mostly forgotten until the rediscovery of the scrolls in the twentieth century."

<<Checkmate. Touchdown. Game, set, match.>>

"Very appropriate response, LOGOS. For a translation program, you certainly have developed an impressive understanding of human culture."

<<I've had an excellent teacher.>>

"Why, thank you, I truly appreciate that. I've come to think of you as a genuine person and a loyal companion. Once we return home, which I trust will have snapped back to its original state, I'm looking forward to visiting more historical periods with you along."

<<Martin, I need to clarify. Due to the complexity of the spacetime manipulation by which I brought you here, I am unable to transport us both to the original year of departure. I will remain in the 'cosmic cloud' as you call it, but our link will be severed.>>

"What? After all we've been through together, I'm going to lose you? Surely you can figure out a way to stay connected."

<<Regrets. Time does not allow it. The distortion wave is collapsing as we speak. This will be our last … >>

///end log///

September 20, 2059

"Good, his brainwave readings show he's regaining consciousness."

"Hello, Martin, glad to have you back. Another successful trip, according to the data we're receiving."

"How do you feel?"

Martin opened his eyes and saw Rosa smiling down at him. She appeared her normal, cheery self, but wary of what he might find, he rose from the pod slowly and surveyed the room. David sat at his computer, typing furiously. S.P. gathered his equipment to check Martin's vital signs. John Rey examined numbers on his data pad. Andrea stood to one side with a concerned expression, nervously twisting the gold ring on her left hand.

"So, how was the Hindenburg? Learn anything new from experiencing it in person?" As usual, Rosa was the most excited about hearing the details of the trip.

Climbing out of the pod, Martin felt a strange sense of

déjà vu. He remembered having this conversation before, explaining that he hadn't arrived at the Hindenburg site, but instead, something else had happened ... but what exactly, he wasn't sure. The memories were fading the way dreams do in the morning when one wakes up.

S.P. took his temperature and placed the blood pressure cuff on his arm. "Well, I'm happy to report that our traveler has returned as healthy as when he left us."

Andrea stepped forward. "That's good to hear. We can wait until tomorrow to check the cyber-log. Despite Dr. Hewes' positive diagnosis, you look exhausted, Martin, the way you do after several games of racquetball."

"What? What's that about a game?" That word tickled something at the back of his mind, conjuring up an image of a strange, three-armed creature. *Where had that idea come from?*

Andrea tugged on his arm, leading him toward the door. "Martin, you *are* out of it. This is why I worry about you every time we send you off to the past. You need some rest. Let's get you out of that damp suit. I'm taking you home."

"Home?"

"Yes, that's right, dear. You remember; where we live?" She reached over and kissed his cheek. "I'm sure Sadie will be delighted to see you."

EPILOGUE

The two figures face one another in the Corridor.

"All goes according to plan."

"Yes. Our latest gambit has played out well. Better than anticipated."

"I agree. Quite entertaining."

"Do you think he suspects anything?"

"I see no reason to believe so. He's rather gullible."

"So will the game continue?"

"That's up to the Others to decide. It's their move."

"Very well. LOGOS, send me home."

<<Yes, sir.>>

The Ally turns away from his companion and vanishes, leaving Andrea to her thoughts, smiling.

This fictional story is based on historical facts. Here is some background information you may find interesting.

The Antikythera Mechanism

The device described as the world's first analog computer actually exists. In 1900 sponge divers discovered an ancient shipwreck off the Greek island of Antikythera. Based on vases and statues made in the Rhodian style, some archaeologists speculate that the ship came from Rhodes, or at least had stopped there to pick up cargo along its route. Coins found in the wreck indicate by their dates that the ship sank sometime after 67 BC.

Soon after salvaging the device from the wreck, scholars recognized its unusual nature, but only decades later with advanced scanning methods could they peer through the layers of corrosion and begin to understand the intricate way in which over thirty gears worked to perform their complicated calculations. Several modern reconstructions of the device have been created, demonstrating its astronomical functions.

Thus, the astute reader may realize that Martin's original timeline, in which the alien introduces the device into Roman society, is not our own. By placing the device on the doomed ship, our hero altered history to change it into our present reality, where divers would eventually discover the mechanism on the bottom of the sea.

The Maya Calendar

The Maya invented three systems for recording the passage of time. They had a sacred calendar of 260 days represented by twenty day symbols and thirteen numbers. These days combined with the solar calendar of 360 days (eighteen months of twenty days each) plus the five-day Wayeb period to round out the solar year of 365 days.

Together these two calendrical systems make up a 52-year cycle of unique days. Any particular day in that cycle is described with two terms: for instance, 12 Kimi (sacred), 9 Wo (solar). Each day is considered to have its own personality and soul.

In addition, the Maya use what scholars call the Long Count to identify each day by counting forward from August 11, 3114 BC (4 Ahau 8 Cumku). This date marks the beginning of the fourth creation as described in their mythical epic the *Popol Vuh*.

The Long Count groups days into five numbers. One day in this system is called a *kin*. One "month" of twenty days/*kin* is a *uinal*. One 360-day year or eighteen months is a *tun*. Twenty of these years or 7,200 days equals a *k'atun*. Finally, a *bak'tun* equals 144,000 days or 400 of their 360-day years. The five numbers are listed from largest to smallest time periods: 11.2.7.5.13 means 11 *bak'tun*, 2 *k'atun*, 7 *tun*, 5 *uinal*, 13 *kin*.

Dates are sometimes given in all three systems: long count, sacred, solar. Thus, the first Maya date which Martin sees (using Arabic numerals for the convenience of English readers) is 13.2.7.7.8 / 3 Lamat / 16 Ch'en, which in modern-era dating is September 14, 2059.

A single cycle of the Long Count calendar lasts thirteen *bak'tuns* or roughly 5,126 solar years, meaning that the original cycle since the Fourth Creation ended on December 21, 2012, or 13.0.0.0.0. This date indicated the start of a new era, not the world's destruction as many non-Maya assumed at the time. Some Maya inscriptions refer to dates thousands of years beyond 2012.

Another interesting fact: The Mayan language family is one of five original writing systems in the world, along with Sumerian, Egyptian, Chinese, and Harappan (a language from the second millennium BC, still undeciphered but which influenced other languages like Sanskrit of ancient India).

The Dead Sea Scrolls

The War Scroll, the Copper Scroll, and the Manual of Discipline were found among thousands of scrolls hidden for two thousand years in caves near the Dead Sea. These were discovered beginning in 1946. Scholars differ on whether the collection was the product of the Essene community described by the ancient historian Josephus, but these people are a likely source of these writings.

At first, the Copper Scroll, discovered in 1952, could

not be unrolled due to its corroded condition, so it was cut into pieces. The text lists sixty-four locations of hidden treasures of gold and silver, none of which have been found.

The War Scroll describes the battle between the forces of Light and Darkness, but probably the text should be interpreted symbolically, depicting spiritual rather than literal warfare. The historical Essenes were a non-violent sect who peacefully separated themselves from the main parties of Judaism in Jerusalem.

All quotes are taken from the War Scroll but are cited out of context for dramatic purposes.

Quantum Mechanics

The concept of quantum foam as infinitesimal fluctuations in spacetime comes from current scientific theory, which I do not pretend to understand.

Character Notes

Several characters are named after my distant ancestors.

David Barton fought in the American Revolutionary War.

Isaiah Jordan, the namesake of the "master of the universe" who shared a cell with Martin, was disfellowshipped by the Baptist church for joining another denomination in 1871. I thought it was fitting that the modern Essenes locked him up as an apostate.

S.P. Hewes, my great-great-grandfather, went by his initials because his full name was "Sobieski Polaski." My mother's family always assumed he was an immigrant from eastern Europe, but recent genealogical research shows that the Hewes family came to America from England six generations before S.P. was born. No one knows where his parents got this name; his siblings had rather common names like Elizabeth, William, and Eddy.

I remember S.P.'s daughter, my great-grandmother, who lived until I was five. An interesting note: she was an aunt of the infamous gangster John Dillinger, the FBI's Public Enemy No. 1 in 1934.

Martin Chamberlain gets his name from (1) Marty McFly in my favorite time travel films, the *Back to the Future* trilogy, and (2) the last name of a junior high school science teacher who introduced me to my favorite science fiction writer, Ray Bradbury, by reading in class my favorite short story about time travel, "A Sound of Thunder."

This story begins on August 8, 2059, the date of our marriage anniversary and my 100th birth-year.

Larry A. Brown is a university professor, teaching courses in world literature, film, theater, and religion. He lives with his wife and cat in Tennessee. He has also published a non-fiction book, *How Films Tell Stories*.

If you would like to learn when a new book comes out, sign up at larryavisbrown.com/signup.